THE CLIQUE

A NOVEL BY
LISI HARRISON

LITTLE, BROWN AND COMPANY
New York ᵔ Boston ᵔ London

To Ken Gottlieb, Shaila Gottlieb, and Kevin Harrison

for always being there with

the right words when I get stuck.

If you like this book, you may also enjoy:
Twilight *by Stephenie Meyer*
The Dating Game *by Natalie Standiford*

Little, Brown and Company
Time Warner Book Group
1271 Avenue of the Americas, New York, NY 10020
Visit our Web site at www.lb-teens.com

First Edition

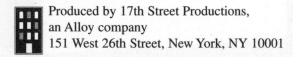
Produced by 17th Street Productions,
an Alloy company
151 West 26th Street, New York, NY 10001

ISBN 0-316-70129-7

10 9 8 7
CWO
Printed in the United States of America

CLIQUE novels by Lisi Harrison:

THE CLIQUE

BEST FRIENDS FOR NEVER

REVENGE OF THE WANNABES

INVASION OF THE BOY SNATCHERS

"Massie, wipe that confused look off your face," Massie's mom, Kendra, said. "It's really very simple—you're not going."

Massie Block flicked the tiny bell that dangled from her gold charm bracelet over and over again. The hollow pings were the only sounds she could make, unless of course she wanted to be accused of "interrupting" by her annoyingly polite mother, which she didn't. She just wanted to win the argument they were having.

"But I have plans and it would be *rude* if I broke them," Massie said. "Right? I mean, haven't you always told me to 'honor my engagements'?" She made air quotes just to remind her mother that the rule was hers in the first place.

Massie looked to her father, William, for backup, but he just sipped his tea and continued reading the latest copy of *Westchester* magazine.

"I told you about this weeks ago," Kendra said. She spoke very slowly and enunciated every word, in much the same way she talked to Inez, their live-in housekeeper. "Your father has been good friends with Mr. Lyons since college. They are moving to Westchester all the way from Florida so that Mr. Lyons can work for him. And while they are looking for a home of their own, they will be living in our guesthouse. And as our daughter it is important that you're here to greet them when they arrive."

"Why?" Massie narrowed her eyes. "They're Dad's freeloading friends, *not mine.*"

Kendra shot her husband a desperate look across the table. William stayed focused on the magazine.

"Well, they'll be your friends soon enough." Kendra said. "Claire is starting the seventh grade on Tuesday too, so you should have plenty to talk about."

"What? Like math?" Massie snapped.

"You can always invite her to join in on your plans," Kendra suggested. "Then you won't miss out on anything."

"Impossible." Massie shook her head. "We've had these appointments for weeks. We can't just call up the spa and add another person at the last minute." Massie looked away. "Not that we'd want to," she said under her breath.

"Then it's settled," Kendra said. "Inez will have brunch on the dining room table tomorrow at 1:15 P.M. Don't be late."

Massie turned and stomped out of the kitchen. Her black pug, Bean, scurried across the floor, trying to keep up without getting too close to Massie's deadly three-inch mules. When they got to the staircase, Massie leaned down and scooped up the puppy with one hand.

Normally she took her heels off before climbing the steps because of the "delicate high-gloss finish on the wood." But considering the circumstances, she chose to leave them on. Every floor-scuffing step would pay her mother back for destroying the Labor Day plans she had with her three best friends.

When she got to the second floor, Massie kicked off her shoes and padded across the plush carpet straight into her bedroom. And slammed the door behind her.

"Don't slam!" came Kendra's voice over the intercom. Massie looked at the white speaker by the bed and rolled her eyes.

Everything in her room was white: the leather chaise by the bay window, the sheepskin rug, the painted brick walls, the dozen fresh tulips, and her flat-screen Mac. Her friends called it the iPad. She'd designed it that way after she stayed in the presidential suite at the Mondrian in Los Angeles. The only color in the enormous hotel room had come from the decorative green apple in the middle of the white marble coffee table. She loved how crisp and orderly everything looked.

But just the other day she'd read in a British gossip magazine that purple was the official color of royalty, which explained the brand new mauve Calvin sheets on her bed. She'd been hoping to buy more in the "queen's color" during her Labor Day shopping spree, but that was no longer an option.

Massie lifted her dog in the air so their eyes could meet. "Bean, tell me this isn't happening."

Bean blinked.

"Missing out on tomorrow could stunt my social growth for the *rest* of the year," Massie said.

Bean licked Massie's thin wrist. She loved the taste of Chanel No. 19.

"Everyone will have a fresh batch of inside jokes I won't even *get*. I'll have to smile like a good sport while everyone laughs and says, 'Oh, you just *had* to be there.'" Massie shook her head vigorously as if her mind was an Etch A Sketch that could erase thoughts she didn't like.

"And you know Dylan will buy the YSL lip markers I put a 'yes' sticker on in *Lucky*," she said. "And you wanna know *why* this is happening?" Massie continued. She didn't wait for Bean's reaction. "So I can meet some girl from Orlando who's going to be living here for a *year*. I mean, what's the urgency? She's not going anywhere." Massie paused and searched her brain for a reasonable explanation. "Unless of course she has a life-threatening illness."

Bean yelped.

"And if she does . . ." Massie let out a heavy sigh. "Why should I get attached?"

Massie ripped up the itinerary she made for her friends that detailed everything she had planned for their day of beauty. She stood above her trash can and let the scraps of paper fall through her fingers like snowflakes. She could see that words like *spray tan, eyebrow wax, aroma* (*therapy* had been torn away), and *Bergdorf's* were still intact.

Massie collapsed on her bed and stretched her arm toward her night table. She grabbed her cell and hit "1" on her speed dial. The girl on the other end picked up after the first ring.

"Heyyy," Alicia said

"Hold on, I'll get Dylan," Massie said.

"'Kay ."

Massie punched in "2" and pressed Send.

"Dyl?"

"Yeah."

"Hold on, I'll get Kristen."

Massie pressed "3."

"Hey, Mass," Kristen said.

"Hey, Alicia and Dylan are here too," Massie said.

"What's up?" Kristen asked. She sounded nervous, like she was about to get blamed for something she didn't do.

"I can't go with you guys tomorrow," Massie blurted.

"Yeah, right." Dylan snorted.

"No, I'm serious. You're not going to believe this, but I have to—" Massie paused and reconsidered her next words. "I have the flu." Which came out sounding like, "I hab da flu."

"Gawd, you sound awful," Kristen said.

"Yeah, maybe we shouldn't go," Dylan offered. "We can come over and take care of you instead."

"What? Not go?" Alicia snapped. "I mean, Massie, what *exactly* is wrong with you? Maybe we can help."

"Feber. Headache. Stuffed up doze, you doh, duh usual." Massie added a sniff and an "uuugggghhh" for effect.

"Dylan's right. We'll bail," Kristen said. "It won't be the

same without you. Who's going to squeeze my hand when I get my eyebrows waxed?"

"And who's going to tell me if I look fat when I try stuff on?" Dylan asked.

"The mirror," Alicia said.

Kristen let out her famous raspy, phlegm-filled cackle.

"Massie, please don't leave me alone with them," Dylan joked.

Massie smiled with relief. They wanted her with them. They *needed* her with them. And that, as always, was all that mattered. But she also knew how quickly they could change their minds.

"You all go. But I want to hear every detail of what happened." Massie momentarily forgot her sick voice. "Every single one."

Unfortunately, the Lyons family arrived right on time. When the doorbell rang, Massie crouched below the banister on the second floor and watched. Her parents were gathered around the Blocks' daughter, Claire.

"Claire! What a knockout you've become," William Block said. He turned to his wife. "Kendra, who does she look like?"

Massie leaned forward to sneak a closer look, but they had already started walking toward the dining room.

"Gwyneth Paltrow!" Kendra announced. Massie thought her mother sounded like an overly excited contestant on a game show.

"Where's *your* gorgeous daughter?" a man's voice asked. Massie assumed it was Mr. Lyons.

"Good question," Massie's mom said.

Massie stood up and tiptoed into her bathroom for one last look at her "first-impression" outfit. She had no intention of becoming friends with Claire but still thought it important to let the girl know what she'd be missing. Massie checked the back of her satin cargo pants for panty lines and examined her white Hermés scarf (worn as a belt, of course) to make sure the knot was sitting flat against her hips. Her white cashmere tank top was free of dog hair and her amber eyes looked bright. No one would ever know she had cried herself to sleep the night before.

"Massie, the Lyonses are here," her mom broadcasted over the intercom.

"'Kay." Massie said into the speaker. She slicked a coat of clear gloss on her mouth, gave her hair a final flip, and made her way toward the dining room.

"There she is!" Judi Lyons had such a big smile, the tops of her chubby cheeks almost touched her eyes.

"Massie!" Jay Lyons reached his arms out to hug her. Massie looked back at him blankly.

"Hey," Massie said. She lifted her right hand and swiveled it from side to side, just like a queen.

William walked around the long oak table and put his arm around his daughter.

"Massie, Jay is my oldest friend," William said.

"Wait a minute, let's not bring age into this," Jay joked.

Everyone burst out laughing except Massie, who glanced at Claire and then quickly looked away. Despite the speedy once-over, Massie managed to detect a pair of overalls, white Keds, and straight blond hair with bangs. She looked like one of the cast members on *Barney and Friends*.

And then she looked to Claire's right and saw Todd, Claire's ten-year old brother, sticking his pudgy fingers in Bean's ears.

"That's my dog, not a baseball glove," Massie barked.

"Todd, leave the dog's ears alone." Jay grinned.

"Sorry about my brother," Claire said in a kind voice. "I'm Claire, the normal one in the family." She extended her hand for a shake. Massie met it with a grip so tight Claire giggled uncomfortably and contorted her body in an effort to get loose.

Claire's arm was covered in a stack of bracelets, obviously homemade. Some were made out of colored beads and others of braided string.

"You okay?" Massie asked. She raised her eyebrows and tipped her head to the side, like she had no idea why Claire was so jumpy.

Kendra clapped once. "All right. Well, why don't we all sit down?" she said. "Jay and Judi can sit over there on William's left." Kendra pointed. Massie noticed that her mother's diamond rings were turned around, which Massie knew meant that the Lyonses didn't have a lot of money. Kendra always did that when she didn't want the "less fortunate" to feel uncomfortable.

"Massie, why don't you sit over there next to Claire," Kendra said.

Massie sat down without making eye contact. She had an idea or two of her own about where her mother should sit.

Once the food was served and everyone was distracted, Massie took out her cell phone and held it under the table. She kept her head up while her thumbs typed a text message.

MASSIE: U THERE?
ALICIA: YEAH
MASSIE: ??? R U DOING?
ALICIA: K IS CRYING.
WON'T LET SVETLANA WAX HER OTHER BROW

MASSIE: WANT ME 2 TALK 2 HER?

Massie moved a stuffed mushroom cap around her plate with her fork while she waited for Alicia to answer.

ALICIA: G2G. FEEL BETTER

Massie's heart started beating quickly. She could picture everyone in Svetlana's tiny waxing room standing around Kristen, laughing hysterically and trying to convince her not to walk out with uneven eyebrows.

Inside joke number one.

Massie decided to send a text message to Kristen anyway. She wanted to be the one to convince her to endure the pain so Svetlana could finish the job.

MASSIE: STAY STRONG. PAIN IS BEAUTY ☺

She glanced down for a spilt second to make sure she got the smiley icon in the right place before she hit Send.

"Massie, no phones at the table," Kendra said.

"Sorry," Massie lied.

"Why don't you take Claire upstairs and show her your room?" Kendra suggested.

"'Kay." Massie glanced down at her cell phone, but Kristen was clearly too busy to type a response. Massie sighed and bit her lip.

"I heard West Chester is like the Beverly Hills of New York," Claire said. She stood in front of the bay window in Massie's bedroom and looked down on the tennis courts, the swimming pool, and the stone guesthouse. She was working hard to sound relaxed, but really, Claire had never been in a private house this big before.

"What's West Chester?" Massie asked. She sounded utterly confused. "Oh, wait, do you mean Westchester?"

"Yeah, isn't that what I said?" Claire turned away from the window and looked back at Massie. She twisted and turned the bracelets on her arm.

"I can't believe you made those in kindergarten and they still fit you," Massie said. "You must have super-tiny wrists."

"I didn't make these in kindergarten." Claire's voice was kind and understanding because she didn't want Massie to feel stupid for making such a ridiculous assumption. "My best friends made these for me when I left Florida." She looked proud. "They also gave me this so I could send pictures of my new school." Claire pulled a tiny silver camera out of the chest pocket on her overalls. "And my new friends," Claire continued. She aimed the lens at Massie and snapped a picture. Massie moved. Claire checked the shot to see if she would have to take it again.

"Oh, it's all blurry." Claire sounded disappointed.

"I'm not surprised," Massie said. "Those cameras pretty much suck."

"Hey, where did you get that cool mannequin?" Claire asked. She was referring to the headless figure that stood on a metal stand by Massie's closet.

"I get a new one every year for my birthday," Massie said. She sounded proud.

"Why every year?" Claire asked.

"Because I grow." Massie gave a tiny eye roll.

"Do you ever think it's going to come to life in the middle of the night and try to murder you?" Claire asked. She tried to sound playful.

"Never," Massie said.

Claire quickly looked around for something new to talk about and walked toward the corkboard that hung above Massie's desk.

"Who are *they?*" Claire noticed that the girls in the pictures looked so much older than her friends back home.

"My best friends in the whole world," Massie said. "We're really close."

"Is this one a model?" Claire pointed to a sultry-looking girl with impossibly glossy dark hair.

"Not that I know of," Massie said. "That's Alicia."

Claire thought Massie sounded bored. Claire saw pictures of the four girls screaming on roller coasters, lying on sleeping bags waving, and dressed up as gun-toting cowgirls. She assumed the costumes were for Halloween because each girl had a line of fake blood dripping from her mouth and Bean wore a cowboy hat and a sheriff's badge. The shot of the girls posing with Santa Claus at the mall made Claire laugh out loud.

"I can't believe you did that to Santa," Claire said. She was referring to the bunny ears Massie was making with her two fingers behind his head.

Massie didn't respond. She was too busy checking her cell phone for messages.

"You guys look like you have a lot of fun together," Claire said. "I can't wait to meet everyone."

Massie lifted her eyes as if she was peeking out over a pair of sunglasses.

"I'm sure you'll meet a bunch of other people you'd rather hang out with."

"Doubt it," Claire said.

"You should definitely try," Massie said. "My friends and I have our own thing going and you'll probably feel weird if you try to join in. You know, because we've known each other for so long."

"I'll be okay." Claire forced a smile. Massie had stopped paying attention.

The phone by her bed rang and she raced toward it as if she had been expecting an important call.

"Uccch, what, Mom?" Massie sounded annoyed.

Claire used this time to take a look around Massie's bedroom.

Her shelves were filled with first-prize horseback-riding trophies and ribbons. In the center of them was a black child-size velvet riding helmet and a framed picture of a white pony.

There was a doggie sleigh bed on the floor that was an exact replica of the human-size one above it.

Massie slammed the cordless phone down on her night table.

"Come on, I have to show you the guesthouse," Massie said.

"It's okay, I can see it from here." Claire pointed at the window. "You don't have to take me."

Massie gestured to the phone. "Actually, I do."

Massie slid open one of her closet doors and Claire saw at least fifty pairs of shoes tucked away in different cubby-holes. Massie tapped her lip with her index finger and examined her selection. She picked out a pair of chunky orange Prada flip-flops and slipped them on her feet.

"Why are you changing?" Claire asked as she picked at the coral polish on her nails. "Aren't we just going in the backyard?"

"'Yeah, but my heels get stuck in the grass and it ruins them." Massie looked down at Claire's feet. "I'd offer you a pair of flip-flops, but you don't care if those get a little muddy, do you?" Massie pointed to Claire's Keds.

Claire didn't know how to respond.

"Didn't think so." Massie shoes slapped against her heels as she shut off the lights and walked out of her room.

Claire picked a pink chip of polish off her nail and watched it land on Massie's white rug. Normally she would have reached down to pick it up, but she decided to leave it. She figured the room could use a little color.

An hour later Massie was sitting next to Isaac, her family's driver, in the plush leather passenger seat of the family Range Rover. They were on their way to Galwaugh Farms, where Massie was going to burn off meeting the Lyons family with a nice long ride on her horse, Brownie, on a private trail.

For the first time all day Massie relaxed. The windows were open all the way and the wind felt good against Massie's face.

"I can't believe that family is taking advantage of Daddy like that," Massie said.

"What do you mean?" Isaac asked.

"Why don't they get their own place? I'm sure there's a YMCA around here somewhere," she answered.

Isaac gave Massie one of his you-did-*not*-just-say-that looks and ejected the "Cheesy Pop" CD from the stereo. Massie knew that meant he was going to say something important.

"I think it's nice that your parents are helping out their old friends. And it's not forever," he explained. "It's just until Mr. Lyons finds a house of his own."

"What's so hard about buying a house?" Massie asked. "Are they poor?" She said "poor" the same way her mother said "fat."

"No," Isaac said. "But not everyone can afford everything they want, exactly when they want it."

Massie was ready for the music again. She pushed the CD back in, but Isaac immediately hit Eject.

"Claire seems really sweet," he offered. "Don't you think?"

"If I wanted someone sweet following me around all day at school, I'd bring Bean," she said.

"Be nice, Massie." Isaac had a trace of warning in his voice.

Massie frowned and turned away from Isaac for the rest of the ride.

The instant the familiar smell of hay and horse poo filled the car, Massie felt her spirits lift. She smiled to herself as they pulled up to the stables.

"Thanks for the ride, Isaac. See you in an hour." Massie slammed the door and ran to the stables to greet her white horse, Brownie.

"Brownie, I have a surprise for you!" Massie swung a Ziploc bag full of carrots in front of the horse's face like a hypnotist. "I washed them, peeled them, and cut them into different shapes." Massie held up an orange star before she fed it to him.

"See?"

Brownie licked her hand with his thick black tongue and Massie hugged him.

She'd gotten Brownie for her fifth birthday and together they'd won eleven ribbons—eight for jumping, two for trotting, and one for best mane.

Massie waited for Brownie to chomp down the last star

before she put her foot through the rhinestone-studded stirrup and hoisted herself up.

She tapped him lightly with her Hermés riding crop, and they started down the manicured trail. The grass that surrounded the dusty path was lush and Hunter Lake shimmered in the not-too-far-off distance. Massie inhaled deeply. The air smelled clean and the farm felt still—like there was no one around for miles.

She was ready to pick up the pace. She triple-tapped Brownie and he began to gallop. Massie could feel her newly sprouted A-cups bouncing along with her. She loved the constant reminder that they were there.

"Brownie, did I tell you I'll be entering the seventh grade as a bra wearer?" she asked.

She didn't mind that Brownie had no idea what she was talking about. He was a good listener, better than her friends and almost as good as Bean.

"There's one thing Claire can't join in on—no matter how hard my mother pushes," she said. "She's even flatter than Kristen."

Massie's one-way conversation with Brownie was cut short when a stranger's voice interrupted her. It was a guy. He was shouting something, but Massie couldn't hear what he was saying.

"I said, on your *left!*" he repeated.

She whipped her head around and screamed when she saw how close his horse was to Brownie. She was about to get pushed off the path and dumped into the ravine that ran vertically alongside the trail. She called it "the gutter" because it reminded her of a bowling alley. But if she landed in it at the speed she was traveling, she might as well call it a grave.

The black horse overtook her, its thunderous hooves drowning out Massie's screams. Brownie was so startled, he stopped unexpectedly and nearly launched Massie straight into the air. Massie pulled tightly on the reins until her horse was back on all fours and standing still.

"Oh my God," she said once she composed herself. "Brownie, are you okay?"

She felt the horse shaking beneath her. A cloud of dust formed behind the mystery man and his horse as they rode on.

"'Scuse me?" She tried to scream, but it came out sounding more like a question.

Massie tried again. "HEY, BRAVEHEART?"

By now he was out of earshot and quickly becoming a blur.

"We didn't win all those ribbons for nothing, did we, Brownie?" Massie quadruple-tapped Brownie with her riding crop and he charged forward. She saw Braveheart head toward the lake. She decided to take the shortcut through the woods and meet him there when he arrived.

"Nobody scares us, right, Brownie?" she said. And off they went.

Her hair slapped against her face and stuck to her lip gloss, but she didn't even bother brushing it back. Brownie jumped over broken tree trunks and splashed through creeks all the way to the mouth of the lake. They got there so fast that Brownie was already drinking when Braveheart showed up. Even from a distance Massie could tell he was shocked to see that she had beaten him there. He dropped his reins and lifted his hands above his head like a surrendering outlaw.

Massie's heart pounded.

"Brownie, what if this guy is a toothless escaped convict?" Massie whispered while maintaining eye contact with the stranger. She gripped her phone just in case she needed to make a quick call to 911.

Braveheart started to get closer. He had shaggy blond hair and tanned, muscular arms. The kind you get from real physical labor, not the gym. When he got close enough, she could see that his eyes were deep blue. He was the cutest toothless escaped convict she'd ever seen, even if he *was* wearing muddy Levi's and a wrinkled white T-shirt. She did her best to pry the hair out of her lip gloss before he got any closer.

"You're on a private trail," Massie said in her best sheriff voice.

"Funny, it doesn't feel very private," he answered.

"It would be if you left."

Massie was temporarily blinded by his Crest Whitestrip smile and she instantly wished she could take back her words. Especially when it occurred to her how cute they would look together at the Octavian Country Day School fall dance.

"Is that any way to treat a guy who just got back into town?" he teased.

"What were you in jail for?" Massie asked.

"Reckless riding." He flashed another smile. "Actually, I was shipped off to boarding school in London. But my dad made me come home when he found out I was partying too much." He shrugged. "I guess he's hoping I'll find total misery this year as a Briarwood Academy freshman."

Massie wanted to ask him why he was sent away in the first place, but she didn't want to seem too eager, didn't want him to think she cared.

She hated herself for not having worn her more flattering brown pants. She'd once read in *Teen Vogue,* "Always try to look your best because you never know who you'll run into."

Teen Vogue *one, Massie zero.*

She leaned over and lovingly mussed the mane on his midnight-black horse.

"Her name is Tricky," he said. "I tell her everything."

"You talk to your horse?" Massie asked. "Don't you think that's a little strange?"

"Not at all. I'm Chris Abeley." He held up his palm like an Indian but smiled like a cowboy.

"I'm Massie Block." Massie hooked a piece of shiny brown hair behind her ear and smiled shyly.

"It's nice to meet you, Massie. Well, I'll get out of your way now so you can have your privacy," Chris said.

"It's okay. You can stay . . . if you want." Massie tried her hardest not to sound desperate.

"And risk having you hunt me down again? No way. I'll

be back next Saturday when this trail is open to the public. Maybe I'll see you then?" Chris winked.

"'Kay," was all she could manage.

"Then it's a date?" he asked. Massie felt a surge of energy blast through her entire body. Chris rode off before she had time to answer.

It was getting close to bedtime.

Massie sat on her white chaise in boy shorts and a cotton tank top. A vanilla-scented candle warmed her room. She was brushing Bean, who had curled up in a tiny black ball beside her. She turned down the TV when she heard a knock on her door.

"Can we come in?" William said.

"Sure," Massie answered.

Her parents walked into her room and sat on the bed.

"Are you all ready for school tomorrow?" William asked.

Massie gestured to the outfit on her mannequin.

"Yup."

It wore a lavender Moschino mini, a gray wide-neck slouchy T-shirt, and silver Jimmy Choo sandals. Even though it was supposed to be seventy-eight degrees tomorrow, her denim blazer was a must. It gave the outfit a finished look.

"Did you end up having a nice day?" Kendra asked.

"Yeah, it was fine," Massie said.

"Good." Kendra sounded pleased. "Isaac will be in the car at 7:45 A.M. to take you to school. So I'll wake you up at 7:00 A.M., okay?"

"'Kay," Massie said. She was relieved that no mention of

Claire had been made and hoped it would stay like that.

"So what did you think of the Lyons family?" William asked. "Claire is great, isn't she?"

So much for that.

"I can't believe you used to be such good friends with Jay," Massie said to her dad. "You seem so different."

William's pleased smile faded and a crinkled brow took its place.

"Kind of like you're Donald Trump and he's Donald Duck," Massie said.

"Give them a chance, okay?" William pleaded. "For me?"

"Maybe Massie will change her mind once she opens this," Kendra said as she handed Massie a small gift-wrapped box. "Take it. They brought it all the way from Florida."

Massie walked over to the bed and accepted the gift. She peeled away the silver wrapping paper slowly, as if she expected something to jump out at her. She lifted the lid on the small cardboard box. Under the cotton square was a tiny silver microphone. She pinched it between her fingers and held it up to the light the way a paleontologist would examine a tiny fossil.

"They got it for your charm bracelet." Kendra smiled brightly. "Isn't that thoughtful?"

"Why a *microphone?*" Massie asked.

"Because you used to want to be a famous singer," Kendra said.

"When I was six." Massie rolled her eyes.

"Well, it's the thought that counts," William said. "Put it on. I think it would look nice between the shoe and the Eiffel Tower."

"I can't wear this—it's silver," Massie said. "Silver and gold are tacky together."

But it was too late. Kendra reached for her daughter's arm and skillfully unfastened the bracelet as if she worked behind the counter at Tiffany & Co. She fastened the microphone (which Massie thought looked more like a lollipop) and clipped the bracelet back on her daughter's wrist.

"It looks great," William said. "They'll be happy to see you wearing it."

Both of her parents gave Massie a kiss good night.

"Now that you're back in school, are we going to resume our nightly walks?" William asked. He was looking at the dog.

"8:15 P.M. Right, Bean?" Massie turned the dog to face her.

Bean lifted her head and looked at Massie.

"She said 'right,'" Massie explained. "G'night."

Her parents closed her bedroom door gently behind them, like they were trying not to wake a sleeping baby.

Massie looked at the eyesore that dangled off her favorite piece of jewelry. Suddenly the bracelet felt more like a handcuff. She slid it off her wrist and placed it beside her bed on the night table. The only thing left to do before she went to bed was enter the day's State of the Union in her PalmPilot.

She'd always kept a record of her life but had never seen the need to waste words in something like a diary, especially since diaries could fall into enemy hands so easily. Instead, when something significant happened, she summed it all up with a simple list.

CURRENT STATE OF THE UNION	
IN	**OUT**
CHRIS	CLAIRE
PUBLIC TRAILS	PRIVATE TRAILS
HORSES	LYONS

When Massie finished her entry, she lifted Bean onto her lap.

"Five more sleeps until I see Chris Abeley again," she said.

She crawled under her duvet, hoping to quiet her mind and get some beauty rest before the first day of school. She clicked the remote control beside her bed and the lights in her room automatically shut off. Only ten more hours until she saw her friends.

Less than a hundred yards away, Claire tossed and turned. She'd thought reading the OCD School handbook would help her relax and feel more comfortable about her first day of school, but it had the opposite effect. It made her realize how little life in Orlando had prepared her for what she was about to experience.

Certain lines that she'd read in the glossy OCD booklet haunted her like a catchy pop song she couldn't get out of her head. Like, *Fashion is a fine art and a true form of self expression . . . which is why OCD prides itself on being an anti-uniform private school. It is a given that all students will take matters of personal style and grooming very seriously.*

Claire flipped the pillow to the cold side and tried to focus on her breathing: in through the nose, out through the mouth. But visions of the high-powered alumni kept her heart racing. *Thirteen Fortune 500 CEOs, seven gold-medal Olympians, four Pulitzer Prize winners, three Oscar winners, two senators, and one secretary of state.* She had no idea what the secretary of state even *did* and prayed she wouldn't be in the same class as a future one because they'd have absolutely nothing to talk about.

Claire kicked the covers off her legs and jumped out of

bed. She took her favorite mushy pillow and crept down the hallway to her brother's room. The sounds of the house were foreign to her and the creaking wood floors made her uneasy.

Todd was fast asleep on his back, his body diagonal across the entire double bed. Claire thought it was funny to see him buried under the frilly grandma blankets that came with the house, but she was too stressed out to giggle. She gently slid him over to one side of the bed and crawled in. His steady breathing made her feel less alone.

A huge lump had set up shop right in the middle of Claire's throat and she could barely swallow her pancakes. The oval wood breakfast table felt big and impersonal, like everything Claire had experienced so far in Westchester. Todd sat across from her, but he felt ten miles away.

Their old breakfast table in Orlando had been a small Formica square. Everyone had their own side and it was cozy. This table didn't even *have* sides.

Unpacked boxes filled the kitchen and the only thing that felt familiar to Claire was the music coming out of the radio—the Westchester version of her mother's favorite lite FM station, which she insisted on playing whenever she cooked.

"Can't we just turn it off? This music is so depressing," Claire said.

"When you have your own house, you can play whatever you want," Judi said.

"This is hardly *your* house," Claire snapped, surprising herself.

Todd looked up at his sister but was too shocked by her comment to pull his arm out of the Raisin Bran box he had been digging through.

"Claire, what is bothering you?" Judi asked.

"Nothing." Claire swirled her fork around her plate and wrote *SOS* over and over again in a puddle of maple syrup.

"Then why did you sneak into my room in the middle of the night?" Todd teased.

"Because there was a spider in my bed," she told him.

"Looks like there was a *crab* in mine." Todd grabbed something small and tossed it at Claire. It bounced off her cheek and landed on the floor.

"Ewww, what was that?" Claire puckered her face like she'd been sucking on a lemon.

"Ammo," Todd whispered, pointing to the Raisin Bran box. "Raisins are great to throw at people in class." He tapped the side pocket on his cords and Claire knew that meant, "There are more where that came from."

"I'm sure you'll be really popular," Claire said.

"Thanks," Todd replied with a smug look on his face, not picking up on the sarcasm. "Want some? Maybe you could throw a few at Massie."

"Why Massie?" Claire said.

"I was listening at the door while you were in her bedroom yesterday," he said. Todd stood up from the table and contorted his body. He was trying to impersonate Massie, but instead he looked and sounded like a cranky old lady. *"My friends and I have our own thing going and you'll probably feel weird if you try to join in. You know, because we've known each other for so long."*

Claire's face turned red. She couldn't believe her younger brother had heard her being humiliated like that.

"Todd, go brush your teeth—the bus will be here in five minutes," Judi said. "We'll talk about this when you get home."

Todd bolted out of the kitchen and ran up the stairs two at a time.

Claire scraped the uneaten pancakes into the trash and put her plate in the sink. She checked her pink G-Force watch. It was 7:55 A.M.

Back in Orlando, Sarah and Sari were probably on the school bus heading down Tuscawilla Road, most likely trading stories about the new wakeboarding tricks they'd mastered over the summer. Some new girl was probably screaming because Bobby Dennet hid a frog in her backpack or something, and amid the hysteria Greasy Mitch was yelling, "Shut up or I'll drive this bus straight into the alligator swamps." Claire would have given anything to be there.

"Claire, your outfit looks great," Judi said.

"Thanks," Claire said. "But do you think it looks fashionable?"

"Sure, white Gap jeans are a classic," she said. "And your sneakers are brand new and just darling."

Claire looked at her platform navy Keds. All of her friends at home had the same ones.

"I understand you're a little nervous because you're starting a new school, but give it a chance," Judi said. "And don't forget, you have Massie on your side."

"That's what you think," Claire said, and then snapped her mouth shut. She walked casually out of the kitchen and into the narrow front hall before her mother could ask what she meant by that.

"Isaac left a message saying you should be outside at eight o'clock, so you'd better go," Judi said. "Don't forget your lunch."

She handed Claire a Powerpuff Girls lunch box. Claire opened it up and put the turkey sandwich, hot Cheetos, and Gummy Feet in her backpack and ditched the empty box on the foyer table. If the rest of the girls acted as grown up as Massie, Claire knew they'd think The Powerpuff girls were K through sixth, *not* seventh.

Claire felt her mom looking at her with concern.

"Hey, sweetheart. What's your last name?" Judi asked with a small smile.

"Lyons," Claire said.

"And what do Lyons do?" Judi prompted.

"Roar," Claire said.

"I can't hear you," Judi said.

"RRROAR!" Claire said. But that old routine felt outdated and childish in her new home.

"That's better," Judi said. She kissed Claire on the forehead and nudged her toward the door.

Claire walked out and something hit her on the back of her head.

"Sure you don't want some raisins?" Todd yelled. "They can't hurt."

"They can if I sit on your chest and force-feed them to your nostrils," Claire shouted over her shoulder.

Claire wished Massie had heard that one because maybe she'd have been impressed.

She stepped outside the house and inhaled deeply. The

smell of cut grass filled the air and the humidity made her think of home. She puffed her bangs up with her fingers and hoped thcy landed like the even bristles on a paintbrush and not like a pile of pickup sticks. She pulled a tube of grape-scented gloss out of her front pocket and swiped it across her lips.

She knew she had about twenty minutes of alone time in the car with Massie and she wanted everything to be perfect.

Isaac waved hello when he saw Claire across the lawn. He was in the driveway buffing the Blocks' silver Range Rover. When Claire arrived, he stuffed the rag in his back pocket and opened the door for her.

"Good morning, Claire," he said with a smile. "Welcome aboard."

"Thanks, Isaac." Claire smiled back. She exhaled deeply. *So far, so good.*

Claire slid across the black leather interior and noticed that it was just as shiny as the car's exterior. She settled in and faced forward, but instead of the car's dashboard, a second row of seats stared back at her. She wanted to stretch out and put her feet on the cushions across from her, but she didn't want Isaac to think she was rude. She decided to wait and see if Massie did it first.

After looking around, Claire felt more like she was in a limo, not a Range Rover. A glass-fronted fridge stocked with diet soda, Pellegrino, Glaceau Vitamin Water, and fresh seasonal berries hummed in the back right corner and a TV shaped like a cube hung from the roof like a disco ball. It had screens on each side so everyone had a view. The tiny black speakers in every corner only added to Claire's feeling that her morning commute would be anything but boring. She was so excited, for a minute she forgot to be nervous but was quickly reminded when she saw Massie marching toward the car.

The tinted windows allowed Claire to study Massie's every move without getting caught.

Massie walked tall and with purpose. Her gaze was fixed, but she didn't seem to be looking at anything in particular.

Claire slid her blond bangs to the side of her forehead to keep the sweat from making them look wet. She envied Massie's perfect hair, dark, shoulder length, and shiny. The kind that always looks good, even first thing in the morning.

Isaac opened the door and a thick gust of heat rushed in. A strappy, feminine sandal and red toenails were the first things in the car. Then the smell of crisp, sweet perfume filled Claire's nostrils. A thin arm that looked like it was about to snap under the weight of a cluttered charm bracelet released a denim blazer into the backseat. It landed on Claire's lap and she quickly placed it neatly beside her. Finally Massie backed herself in and slid across the entire seat. She bumped into Claire's knee.

"Oh my God!" Massie said. "You scared me. What are you doing in here?"

"What do you mean?" Claire asked. "Your mom said I should ride with you to school." She quickly thought about how Isaac had greeted her. He'd seemed to know she was coming. "Didn't she tell you?"

"Sorry," Massie said. She inched over to the other side. "I must have forgotten."

"Oh," Claire said.

Isaac started the engine and both girls studied his every move, as if they'd never seen someone drive a car before. They didn't know where else to look.

"This sure beats the school bus," Claire said.

"I wouldn't know, but I'll take your word for it," Massie replied. She looked at the screen of her cell phone. "Claire, you wouldn't mind sitting in the very back, would you? We have to pick up Alicia, Kristen, and Dylan and I would hate for it to get too squished up here." Massie looked directly into Claire's eyes. "I guarantee it will still 'beat the school bus.'" Her air quotes were sharp and full of attitude.

"Oh, I thought it was just going to be us," Claire said.

"Why would you think *that?*" Massie asked.

Claire was too stunned to answer. Instead she did what she was told and crawled over her seat and into the back section of the car, the same one she assumed was for transporting cargo or pets. It only took her a second to notice that her new seat offered an obstructed view of the TV screen and no access to the fridge.

After a few minutes the Range Rover pulled off the road and stopped. Claire felt confused. All she could see were tall iron gates and overgrown bushes behind them. Claire moved closer to the window and squinted so she could figure out what needed so much protecting, but she could only make out a naked woman carved out of stone and a marble fountain.

Claire fished around the inside of her knapsack and pulled out her tiny camera. She snapped a picture of the iron gates and then one of a security guard.

"Claire," Massie said. She didn't bother turning around. "This isn't Epcot."

Her name came out more like "Kuh-laire" the way Massie said it.

"If the guards know you're taking pictures of the house, they'll confiscate your camera and question you for a week straight," Massie said.

"Oh my God, I'm so sorry. I've just never seen anything—"

"Well, don't advertise it," Massie said. "Everyone lives like this around here, so you better get used to it."

Finally a dark-haired girl emerged from behind the gates. She glided toward the car slowly and casually. She didn't seem the least bit concerned that everyone had been waiting for her. When Claire got a closer look at her, she understood why.

Alicia was the most beautiful girl she'd ever seen. The kind no one ever gets mad at because they don't want her looking unhappy. Her dark brown eyes sparkled brightly against her perfectly even tan, and her lips were full and cherry red.

"She's in vintage Ralph Lauren and has the new Prada messenger bag," Massie said.

"What?" Claire asked. She had no idea what Massie was talking about. She leaned forward and asked again, "What?"

"'Kay, we'll be at your house in five minutes," Massie

said into her phone. "Bye." Massie snapped it shut and tossed it in a cup holder.

Claire's face turned red when she realized that Massie hadn't been talking to her.

Isaac opened the door and Alicia Rivera slid in beside Massie.

"Heeeyyyyy," Massie said, squeezing her friend.

Alicia took a long look at Massie.

"Ehmagod, you don't look like you were sick at all," Alicia gushed. "You look ah-mazing."

"Just wait for tomorrow," Massie said.

"Why?" Alicia asked with a sly grin.

"Because I get better looking every day!" they shouted in unison at the top of their lungs. They cracked up and high-fived each other. Even Claire had to laugh at that one.

Alicia whipped her head around to the back of the car to see where the extra sound came from.

"Who's the stowaway?" she asked.

"Oh, we're just giving her a ride today. Her family is staying in our Guesthouse until they can afford a place of their own," Massie said.

"Hi, I'm Claire," she said, trying to ignore the sting of Massie's comment.

"Oh," Alicia said.

Claire unzipped her knapsack and took out a bag stuffed with gummy worms and sours.

"Want some?" she asked. She used her teeth to untie the tight plastic knot she had made extra tight when she took them out of her lunch box. "I live on them."

"I stopped eating those around the same time I stopped breastfeeding," Massie snapped.

"Yeah, and I never started," Alicia said.

Claire dropped the bag back in her knapsack and tried not to think about how badly she wanted to chew on a sour foot. She leaned her head against the window and counted the trees as they passed by.

The car slowed down in front of a tall white A-frame that sat on top of a small hill. It looked more like a church than someone's home. This time Claire managed to snap a picture of the manse without getting busted by security or worse—Massie.

Dylan Marvil was perched on the stone steps in front of her house reading *Us Weekly* and eating a nutrition bar. A thick mass of fiery red hair blew around her pale face, which she was fighting to keep away from her mouth so she could eat. When she saw the Range Rover, she stuffed the magazine in her Louis Vuitton backpack and ran down the remaining steps.

Dylan was at least two inches taller and wider than the other two girls. Claire thought she looked like a girl who'd grown up milking cows or churning butter on a farm.

Dylan's entrance into the car was a lot less graceful than Alicia's. The strap on her bag got tangled around the door handle and her left mule slid off her foot and under the car.

"We missed you yesterday," Dylan said as she hugged Massie. "How are you feeling?"

Massie turned her head slightly toward the backseat. It was the second time she had looked at Claire all morning.

"Better," Massie said. "So whadja buy?"

"Not much. Just three pairs of jeans, a cashmere sweater I'm not even sure I like, and a couple of Calvin dresses for bar mitzvah season." She took a brush out of her backpack and worked it through her long hair.

"You should have seen her try to walk in five-inch Manolos," Alicia said. "Her entire body shook like she was in a giant earthquake."

Dylan cracked up.

Massie opened the minifridge and looked inside. She seemed just as bored by berries and beverages as she was by her friends talking about their shopping adventures.

"Shut up," Dylan said. "At least I didn't get felt up by the bra lady."

Alicia gave Dylan a wide-eyed look that was one part surprise and two parts amusement. "You promised you weren't going to tell anyone."

"I didn't think you meant *Massie*," Dylan said. "Hey, Massie, don't you think that was worth at least two gossip points?"

"Sorry," Massie said. "I wasn't even listening."

Claire could tell by Massie's sudden change in mood that she didn't like feeling left out, almost like she took it personally when people had fun without her.

"Didn't you get something at the cosmetics counter?" Alicia added.

Dylan shot her a "thanks a lot!" look that Claire noticed all the way from the backseat.

"Oh yeah, I also got an Yves St. Laurent lip marker," Dylan confessed.

"Oh, like the one I said I wanted?" Massie said coolly. "Be careful, I read they cause cold sores."

"Come on! Where did you read that?" Dylan said with a tinge of fear in her voice.

"I think it was *YM*," Massie said.

Dylan held the back of her silver brush up to her face and tried to catch her reflection. She pressed her tongue against the inside of her top lip so she could get a closer look.

"I don't see anything," Dylan said.

"I smell airplane food. Does anyone else smell that?" Massie asked.

"It's me," Dylan said. "There's a Zone lunch in my backpack."

"When did you start the Zone diet?" Alicia asked. She sounded genuinely interested.

"Today. My mom and my sisters are doing it too. We all want to lose fifteen pounds by Halloween," Dylan said.

"The smell alone will keep you from eating," Massie said.

"Seriously," Alicia agreed.

The last stop before school was the Montdor to pick up Kristen. She sat hunched over in the dimly lit lobby of the luxury building, working on a crossword puzzle. Her long dirty blond hair covered her face. Isaac had to honk twice before she finally jumped up and pushed her whole body against the heavy revolving door in order to get outside.

Kristen Gregory was one of those people who bounced when she walked. Her tiny frame was made up entirely of muscle, just like Claire's. Finally, someone she could relate to. Claire decided she liked Kristen the best so far. Like the others, she was dressed head to toe in designer wear. But her choices were pure comfort food. Orange Puma sneakers and chocolate brown velour sweats and a matching hoodie with the sleeves pushed up.

"Heyyy," she said as she jumped into the car and hugged each girl. "We missed you yesterday, Mass."

When the Range Rover was in motion, Kristen slid off her sweats to reveal a short jean mini and a belly shirt.

"My gawd," Massie said as she watched Kristen struggle. "When is your mom going to let you wear what you want?"

"Puh-lease, I stopped asking that question years ago. At this point it's much easier for me to live a double life," Kristen said. She stuffed her sweats under the seat.

"Let's give Massie her prezzy," Alicia said. She searched the inside of her bottomless Prada bag.

"Wait, before we do, I have two questions," Kristen said. "One, why does the car smell like American Airlines, and two, who is that in the backseat?"

Dylan looked over her shoulder and screamed at the top of her lungs when she saw Claire.

"Ohmygod, who is *that?*" She paused to catch her breath before she continued. "Massie, has she been here the whole time?" Dylan asked.

Massie rolled her eyes and nodded.

"Her name is Claire. Her family is living with Massie until her dad can make enough money to get his own house. She's in our grade at OCD," Alicia said with a proud smile.

Claire could tell by the way Alicia sat up and raised her voice when she explained Claire's "situation" that she loved being the first person Massie picked up in the morning. It meant she got updated before anyone else, and that seemed to be really important to her.

Kristen extended her hand toward the backseat and shook the air.

"Sorry for the virtual handshake, but I can't reach you all the way back there. I'm Kristen."

Claire stuck her hand out and shook the air too, but Kristen had already turned her attention back to the other girls.

"I can't believe she's been sitting back there this whole time," Dylan mumbled. She started to brush her hair again.

Claire watched as strands of red hair landed on the back of her lime green Izod.

KRISTEN: DO WE LIKE HER?
MASSIE: 👎 .

Massie let out a sigh and stretched her arm across the backseat, like a boy trying to "get some" off his date during a movie. Obviously Massie wanted her to see her tiny cell phone display. When Claire saw the thumbs-down icon, her blood boiled and her body froze.

Claire reached for her bag of gummies and poked a hole in

the side because she didn't want anyone to notice her struggling with the knot. She pulled two worms out and held them behind her back. When she was sure no one was looking, she coughed and popped them in her mouth. They tasted like home.

"'Kay, time to show Massie what we bought her yesterday," Kristen said. "It's a get-well gift from all of us."

Alicia pulled a rectangular slab of white tissue from her bag and handed it to Massie. Dylan clapped excitedly. Massie tore the paper off and threw it over her shoulder toward the backseat. The crumpled white ball landed two inches away from Claire's feet.

"No way! The Alberta Ferretti halter I saw in *Lucky!*" Massie said. "And it's purple, my new favorite color."

"Leesh," Dylan said as she dove toward the halter. "You left the price on." She yanked the dangling tag before Massie could see it and tossed it away like a Frisbee. It landed next to the tissue. Claire looked down to see how much the flimsy top cost. When she saw the numbers, she gasped. She'd never really believed that people "gasped" until that moment.

How can a top thinner than toilet paper be that *expensive?* she thought. The girls were too busy accepting Massie's thank-you hugs to notice Claire, who grabbed the tag off the floor and held it up to her face. It said seven hundred and eighty dollars. $780.00!!! She took out her camera and snapped two shots—one wide and one zoom. No one back home would ever believe this.

Dylan reached for the remote control and flipped through the TV channels. She stopped on *The Daily Grind.*

"My mom is interviewing cute coma guy from the *Young and the Restless* today," Dylan said with pride. "Shhh, here it is." She leaned forward in her seat.

"Well, Drew, it's been great talking to you this morning. Thank you so much for stopping by. We're all praying you recover from that nasty coma soon so you and your mistress, Melanie, can figure out what to do with your wife's body," Merri-Lee Marvil said. And then she kissed the chiseled blond actor goodbye.

When he was out of the shot, she looked straight into the camera and asked, "Do you ever wonder what your dog *really* thinks of your friends? Canine specialist Dr. Gabby will tell you as soon as we get back from the break."

Dylan angrily shut off the TV.

"I can't believe we missed cute coma guy," Dylan said. "What's his last name again?"

"I think it starts with a *D,*" Kristen said. "Six letters."

"Is everything a crossword puzzle with you?" Massie asked.

"Divine," Claire said. "His last name is Divine."

For one brief moment Kristen must have forgotten that she wasn't supposed to like Claire because she turned around and spoke directly to her.

"That's right," Kristen said. "Thank God, that would have bothered me all day."

"Kristen, don't you think Dylan should swipe cute coma guy's phone number from her mom's PalmPilot?" Massie asked.

Kristen had to turn away from Claire to answer.

"Uh, sure," Kristen said. "Dylan, do you think you can?"

"Given!" Dylan said, as if she was insulted that her friend even had to ask. "We'll be prank calling him by this time tomorrow morning."

"Wait, your mom knows Drew Divine?" Claire asked. She leaned as far forward as she could without falling into the next row of seats. "How?"

"She just spoke to him," Alicia said. "Weren't you watching?"

"Your mom is Merri-Lee Marvil?" Claire asked. "The host of *The Daily Grind?*" *The Daily Grind* was Claire's mother's favorite morning show.

"Uh-huh," Dylan said. She picked an imaginary piece of lint off her top and flicked it into the air.

"Do you get to meet famous people all the time?" Claire asked. "Does she look the same in real life as she does on TV? Is she really dating Geraldo Rivera?"

"That will be all for now, Barbara Walters," Massie said.

Claire fell back into her seat as if she had just been punched in the stomach. She decided not to say anything anymore. What was the point? She just looked out the window and ignored the four girls, who were draped all over each other in a heap of expensive bags, shoes, and clothes.

Massie tuned in to the crunching sound coming from the backseat. She tried to block it out of her head, but it kept getting louder. The faint smell of salt and greasy potatoes filled the air and Massie realized that Claire was eating chips, with no regard for the early hour or the high fat content. Massie pulled out her cell phone like she was drawing a sword.

MASSIE: SHE'S G2G
ALICIA: SO DO HER BANGS
DYLAN: H8 THE WHOLE HAIRCUT
MASSIE: ✓ OUT THE SHOES

Dylan, Alicia, and Kristen turned toward the backseat and at the same time lifted themselves up so they could get a good look at Claire's feet. Massie was dying to see Claire's reaction, but she didn't have the heart to look.

KRISTEN: BETTER DEAD THAN KED
MASSIE: NOT A G.L.U.
DYLAN: ??????

MASSIE: GIRL LIKE US. NEW TERM
DYLAN: LOVE IT!

Massie slipped her phone back in its Prada nylon case, signaling the other girls that it was time to switch back to speaking.

Claire's eyes widened when she saw the school she was expected to go to for the next ten months. The parking lot was filled with Mercedes, Jaguars, Lexus SUVs, BMW convertibles, and even a few limos. Her old school just had yellow school buses and a few beat-up Toyotas and Hondas that belonged to the teachers.

Her mouth started to taste like pennies, which usually meant she was about to puke. She tried to calm down by quietly singing the words to "These Are a Few of My Favorite Things," from *The Sound of Music*—it worked for the von Trapp family and it had always worked for her.

Raindrops on roses
And whiskers on kittens . . .

The massive brick buildings looked much more welcoming on the cover of the brochure. Tangles of green vines swirled up the walls all the way to the roof and tall pine trees surrounded them at the base. Claire figured the excessive greenery was nature's way of keeping out the riffraff.

The instant the car's engine shut off, the girls were on the move. They walked beside each other in a straight line toward the great lawn that spilled out in front of the school's entrance. Tight clusters of friends wearing slight variations of the same outfit were getting reacquainted after the summer break. Mostly everyone wore dark jeans or minis with a tank. The color and cut of the tops seemed left up to the individual, but everything else looked predetermined by the pages of *Teen Vogue*, *Elle Girl*, and *Lucky*. No one had Jansport knapsacks. Instead they carried handbags with designers' initials stamped all over them.

Claire thought it was funny how OCD was an anti-uniform private school, yet all the students dressed exactly the same. Thanks to her mother's idea of "fashionable," she was the only one who stood out.

Bright copper kettles
And warm woolen mittens . . .

She took it all in while she waited patiently for someone to open the back door and let her out of the Range Rover. The clock on the dashboard said 8:30 A.M., which meant she only had ten minutes to find her first class. Isaac cranked up the volume on the stereo, sending loud classical music to every corner of the car, and before Claire knew it, they were moving.

"Isaac," she shouted from the back.

He kept driving.

"ISAAC!" Claire tried again.

She lifted her leg over the seat and crawled into first class. She tapped Isaac on the shoulder.

"Isaac," Claire said, "unfortunately I have to get out."

He jumped and slammed on the brakes. "What are you doing here?"

"That seems to be the question of the day," Claire said.

Isaac reversed the car back into the school's circular driveway.

"Thanks for the ride," Claire said. Isaac closed the door after she stepped out.

But Isaac didn't answer. He was too busy searching the lawn for Massie.

He spotted her hugging an eighth-grade girl with a scooter helmet in one hand and a yoga mat in the other.

"Massie," Isaac shouted. He obviously didn't mind attracting attention because he screamed her name three more times.

Everyone looked his way except Massie.

He abandoned the Range Rover in the middle of the driveway despite the angry drivers who honked and demanded he move it.

"I have to talk to you," he said.

Massie was still speaking to the eighth-grade girl. Dylan, Alicia, and Kristen waited patiently for her to finish so they could move on.

"Massie!" Isaac said.

"What?" she said.

She looked at her friends and rolled her eyes.

"You left Claire in the car." He sounded annoyed.

Massie and the girls let out a snicker.

"I thought *you* were going to let her out," Massie said. She smiled when she spoke.

More giggles.

Claire felt everyone's eyes on her. She wanted desperately to tell them that she had been fine with being left in the car, that it was an honest misunderstanding, and that she'd in no way put Isaac up to this, but she didn't. She sang to herself instead.

Brown paper packages tied up with strings.
These are a few of my favorite things. . . .

"I expect you to treat Claire with kindness and respect." Isaac looked straight into Massie's amber eyes.

"Uh, I better go," the eighth-grade girl said. "Good luck with your babysitting job." Claire watched her run toward her friends like she couldn't wait to tell them what happened. Massie crossed her arms and stared back at Isaac.

"Thanks a lot," Massie said. "She'll probably get at least fifty gossip points for this story." She watched the eighth-grade girl laughing with her friends in the distance and pointing her out. Then she turned her attention back to the driver. "Isaac, did I ask you to take my temperature?"

"What?" Isaac asked. "No."

"Then why are you all up in my butt?" Massie asked.

"Oooh, no, you didn't," Alicia said.

Dylan, Kristen, and Alicia whooped and hollered in celebration of Massie's never-ending cleverness. They exchanged high fives in her honor.

Even Claire couldn't help but be a little bit impressed. Everything Massie said was so smart and funny and *cool.*

Claire looked up at Isaac. She had no idea how he was going to react. She sort of expected him to pull Massie aside and yell or threaten to tell Massie's parents, but he didn't. He just stood tall and stared down at her. Massie stared straight back. It seemed like they were communicating telepathically using their own private language. Everyone watched in silence.

"Fine." Massie took off toward school and Claire followed. Isaac watched from a distance.

"This is OCD," Massie explained in a monotone voice. She sounded like a tour guide who had given the same spiel at least fifty times earlier that day.

"When you get inside, you'll see rows of kiosks that look like ATM machines," Massie continued. "Put your student ID card in and your schedule will pop out. The café is to the left along with the gym, the dance studios, the pool, and the spa. On your right are the seventh-grade classrooms and the teachers' lounge. Meet us here at exactly 3:25 if you want a ride home. If you're not here, we'll assume you decided to walk."

```
┌─────────────────────────────────────────────┐
│                                               │
│        OCTAVIAN COUNTRY DAY SCHOOL            │
│           THE STARBUCKS KIOSK                 │
│              11:25 A.M.                        │
│             September 2nd                      │
│                                               │
└─────────────────────────────────────────────┘
```

Second period had just ended and the girls met at the newly renovated on-campus café for chai lattes before their next class. The café was beautifully done up, complete with cherrywood paneling and brass accents. Kristen carefully grabbed the hot tea from the guy in the Starbucks booth and walked toward Massie, Dylan, and Alicia. They were leaning against a wall mural of people drinking hot beverages throughout history, their hands filled with notebooks, pocketbooks, and venti-size cups.

A gaggle of studious girls dressed in different-colored Juicy sweat suits sped up and looked at the floor as they walked past Massie.

"Look, it's the Mathletes," Massie said. "Cheer up, girls, school has finally started again."

They knew better than to respond.

Alicia leaned toward her friends and whispered, "I think Jena Drezner is wearing her dog's shirt by mistake. Look." She pointed. "It barely covers her rib cage."

"Hi, you guys," Jena said. "How was your summer? You all look so amazing, as usual. Hey, Massie, I heard you're taking that new girl under your wing."

"What?" Massie said.

"Yeah, everyone's saying you have a new BFF," Jena said. "I

was hoping I could meet her. It's been a while since we've had a real 'fashion don't' around here. I've almost forgotten what one looks like. But if anyone can whip her into shape, you can."

"Check your source, Jena. Obviously if I had a new BFF, she'd be here right now." Massie rolled her eyes and took a sip of her latte.

When the girl left, Massie leaned in close to her friends and whispered, "I heard she peed in her bed at sleepover camp this summer."

"I heard the same thing," Alicia said.

"Too bad, I said it first, so I get two gossip points," Massie said.

But Massie had gotten a lot more than a few points from her encounter with Jena. She'd gotten tipped off to the fact that people were talking about her and Claire.

"My social life is in a state of emergency," Massie said under her breath.

"You're not really going to be friends with Claire," Alicia said. "Are you?"

"Yeah," Massie said. "I'm dumping you and bringing her on full time."

"Are you serious?" Alicia asked. Her smile faded. A look of sheer horror took its place. "Is it because I didn't want to cancel our shopping trip to take care of you yesterday? 'Cause I was only kidding."

"I know, so was I," Massie said.

She watched Alicia cross her arms in front of her chest like she had just caught a chill, but Massie knew she was hiding her big boobs. She always did when she got nervous.

"Burberry cap," Massie said. She pointed at a seventh grader wearing a hat made of the signature plaid. "No punch backs." Massie hit Kristen on the arm as hard as she could.

"Owwwww!" Kristen yelped. Her books fell to the floor and the scalding chai latte covered her chest and left arm.

The first person to spot someone wearing anything made by Burberry got to punch whoever they wanted as hard as they wanted. That was the rule. They had been playing this for the last two years and had all suffered a painful blow at one time or another.

Massie heard the familiar squeak of rubber against the floor. Her entire body tensed up. That high-pitched sound meant Claire and her Keds were getting closer.

"Kristen, are you okay?" Claire asked.

"She's fine. We do this all the time. See?" Massie pointed to Kristen, who forced a smile.

"Always come prepared," Kristen said. She lifted a backup shirt out of her bag as if she was pulling a tissue out of a box. She patted her notebooks dry with the hem of the stained T-shirt she was wearing.

Massie could not believe Claire was still standing with them. "Claire, did I invite you to my barbecue?" Massie asked, her neck tilting to the right and her arms tightly crossed.

"Huh? No. I mean, I don't know," Claire said.

"Then why are you all up in my *grill?*" Massie said through her teeth.

Everyone laughed except Claire. Her lower lip twitched.

The piercing sound of the bell jump-started the slow walkers who were shuffling to third period, and suddenly everyone was on the move.

"Gotta go," Dylan said as she bolted to English.

"Think I have time to run to the bathroom and wash the chai off my chest before second bell?" Kristen asked.

"Yeah, go. I'll save you a seat," Alicia answered.

"Hurry," Kristen shouted.

"She doesn't know *how* to hurry," Massie joked.

"Why should I get all sweaty over an art class?" Alicia said.

"I have art too! Is your teacher Vince—?" Claire was cut off.

"You better go, Alicia," Massie said while looking right at Claire.

Alicia sauntered off.

Massie and Claire were left alone to face each other. The hall was suddenly silent and empty. Massie realized this was the first time she had ever looked at Claire's face head-on. She was pretty in a plain sort of way, and Massie couldn't help thinking that with a new wardrobe, a little mascara, and longer bangs she might be able to make a few friends of her own.

"I don't understand why you hate me so much." Claire's voice was shaking.

"Claire, this isn't *Clueless,* okay?" Massie snapped. "Why don't you just make your own friends and worship me from afar like everyone else?"

Claire's aqua blue eyes widened with disbelief and she let out a nervous giggle.

"I practically live with you, Massie," Claire said. "I can't just go away. No matter how hard you try to make me."

"You obviously haven't seen me try," Massie said.

Claire pushed the stack of bracelets away from her wrist and back up her arm. She looked like she was rolling up her sleeves before a fistfight.

"I was just wondering," Claire said. "Are you a female dog?"

"What?" Massie asked. "Why?"

"Because you're acting like a real *bitch!*" Claire shot her a scowl and hurried away before Massie had time to answer.

Poor Claire, Massie thought. *In her world that was probably clever.*

But in Massie's world it was a big mistake.

MASSIE: CLAIRE CALLED US BITCHES
DYLAN: ????
DYLAN: HOW RUDE. SHE JUST MET US
MASSIE: I VOTE HER OFF THE ISLAND
ALICIA: DONE ☺
DYLAN: DONE ☺
KRISTEN: AND DONE ☺

Massie clicked her phone shut and smiled. She knew her friends would do most of the dirty work, which was exactly what she wanted. That way she'd be "innocent" when her mother and her conscience caught up with her for what they were about to do.

When Claire finally got to class, everyone was seated and calm except her.

Vases of colorful flowers lined the window ledges, and bowls of overly buffed fruit filled the shelf along the back wall. The skylights on the ceiling allowed sunny brightness to flood the room, creating a pleasant and cheery environment.

"You look confused, dear. What's your name?" asked a tall thin man in a navy smock that said, DON'T MESS WITH PERFECTION.

The entire class stared at Claire.

"I'm not confused, I'm just looking for a seat," Claire answered. She could feel her face turning red.

"And you arrrrrrre?" He tapped his clog impatiently while he waited for an answer.

"I'm Claire."

"Hello, Claire, I'm Vincent. My likes are swing dancing and must-see TV. My dislikes are . . . let me think . . . hmmm . . . oh, I know—TARDINESS!" he shouted. "So if you would please just grab that seat by the window, I would greatly appreciate it."

The vacancy was beside Alicia, whose vintage suede blazer was already on the free chair to ward off newcomers.

"This isn't the changing parlor at Saks, Ms. Rivera,"

Vincent said. He batted the air with the side of his hand like he was shooing away a mosquito.

Claire slowly made her way through the maze of easels and stools, scanning the room to see if maybe there was another seat she could claim. Alicia shook her head forebodingly, hoping to prevent Claire from coming any closer. All Claire could do was shrug and hope Alicia understood that she had no choice.

Alicia's manicured index finger pointed at the empty space in front of Vincent's desk, but it was too late.

"Claire, I've seen paint dry faster," Vincent said. "Chop chop."

He put his hands on his hips and cocked his head like he was about to toss out another zinger. But the door burst open and his attention was diverted.

The entire class turned to look at the source of the latest interruption while Claire used the opportunity to settle into her seat.

Kristen stood in front of the room, panting like a dog. Her hair was halfway out of her ponytail and she looked frazzled.

"Sorry, Vincent, I was in the bathroom," Kristen said.

"Another tardy, Ms. Gregory, and I will personally hack off that precious blond hair of yours and have it spun into paintbrushes."

Claire was the only one who laughed openly at his threat. Vincent's narrow, pointy face softened when he heard her giggle, and the twinkle in his eye suggested that he was thankful one of his students finally got his sense of humor.

Kristen twisted the loose strands of hair around her finger. She shot Alicia a confused look.

"Where's my seat?" Kristen mouthed.

Alicia tilted her head in Vincent's direction and signaled with her arms that there was nothing she could do about Claire.

"Looks like the only space left is this one," Vincent said, patting the top of the empty stool in front of his desk. His gold pinky ring made a loud tapping sound every time it hit the wooden seat.

Claire scanned every one of her fingernails looking for something to bite, but she had nothing left.

Vincent pulled an egg timer out of his side pocket and set the dial for fifteen minutes. Then he sashayed over to the podium in the middle of the room and grasped the corner of the sheet that covered it. With a quick flick of the wrist he whisked it away, revealing three bright red tomatoes in a bowl.

"You have exactly fifteen minutes to paint a still life called *Ripe Vine Tomatoes*," he explained. "Now begin."

The room was quiet except for the occasional sound of brushes swishing around in water and getting knocked against the sides of cleaning dishes.

Vincent paced up and down the aisles, eyeing everyone's work with the intense scrutiny of an art critic. His ticking egg timer reminded Claire of Captain Hook from *Peter Pan*. She found it hard to focus.

She figured Alicia was distracted too because she was looking around the room nervously. While Vincent commented on someone's "erratic brushstrokes," Alicia turned toward Claire's desk.

"Can I borrow some of your red? Mine's a little clumpy," she said.

"Sure," Claire said.

Alicia leaned over and dunked her brush. She lost her balance on the way up and was forced to grab on to Claire so she wouldn't fall down.

"Sorry about that." Alicia looked slightly embarrassed.

"Are you okay?" Claire asked.

"Yeah, thanks," Alicia said.

"Problem, ladies?" Vincent asked.

"No," they answered in unison.

Claire returned to her still life.

"Four minutes left," Vincent announced.

Alicia burst out laughing.

"Did I miss something funny on *Leno* last night, Ms. Rivera?" Vincent asked.

"No, Vincent, sorry. I think the smell of the paint is starting to get to me. Maybe I should sit down for a minute."

"Good idea," Vincent said as he gently polished one of the model tomatoes with his sleeve.

Claire raced to finish her third tomato but was distracted by another noise. The faint sound of clicking buttons filled her ears and reminded her of the horrible ride to school that morning. They were talking about her again.

KRISTEN:?
ALICIA: •
KRISTEN:???
ALICIA: •
KRISTEN:???!!!
ALICIA: • = CLAIRE GOT HER PERIOD

When Kristen received that final text message, she craned her neck around to sneak a peek at Claire. Sure enough, a big red splotch was on the back of Claire's white jeans. Alicia held up a paintbrush that had been dipped in red paint and waved it around. Kristen put her hand over her mouth, but no palm could conceal her throaty laugh.

When art was over, Claire got up and headed toward the door. Each girl she passed let out a giggle. Claire wiped her hand across her nose to check for loose boogers but didn't find anything. She tousled her bangs in case they were doing that weird split-down-the-middle thing she hated. But people still snickered. Claire was halfway out the door when Vincent stopped her.

"Claire, can you please stay behind for a second?" he asked.

Great, Claire thought.

Cream-colored ponies and crisp apple strudels
Doorbells and sleigh bells
And schnitzel with noodles . . .

"What, dear?" Vincent asked.

"Nothing," Claire said. She hadn't realized she was singing out loud this time.

He scribbled something on a small white notepad and Claire thought he looked like a doctor writing out a prescription.

"I want you to go see the nurse right away," he said. "Take this slip; it will excuse you for being late to your next class."

"Why? What is it?" Claire asked.

"I'd rather the nurse deal with it. Now go," he commanded.

Claire stood and stared at him.

"*Go!*"

Claire raced out of the room but had no idea where she was going. In all of the uncertainty she'd forgotten to ask where the nurse's office was.

Alicia and Kristen were halfway down the hall. Alicia had been so normal, almost *nice* when she'd borrowed the paint. Maybe it'd be okay to ask them.

"Hey, would you guys mind telling me where I can find the nurse?" Claire asked, trying to sound desperate. Maybe if they thought her appendix was bursting or she was running to get help for a dying teacher or something, they would just give her a straight answer without saying anything to her about the saved seat.

"Ehmagod, sure. Just go down the stairs, make a quick right, and walk all the way down the hall to the very end. The office is the last door on your left." Kristen pointed.

Claire felt a little rush of relief. Her dramatic plea had worked like a charm.

"Got it, thanks." Claire took off toward the stairs like

she was Dr. Monica Quartermaine on *General Hospital.*

When Claire was out of their sight, she slowed down and walked. Whispers seemed to follow her wherever she went.

On her way down the stairs she felt a light object hit her butt. She immediately thought of her brother and his raisins. Two more objects knocked her back, but she didn't stop moving. She couldn't. There was a lot of stairwell traffic behind her and she didn't want to stop the flow.

The basement was dim and quiet. It smelled like chemicals. She knocked lightly and waited for an answer.

"Hello?" Claire said as she peeked inside. The room was dark except for a red light that glowed in the corner.

"*Close the door!*" someone barked.

"I'm looking for the nurse," Claire said.

"This is a darkroom!" someone snapped. "The nurse is on the main floor. Next to the art studio."

"Thanks. Sorry." Claire closed the door and dashed back to the stairwell. On her way back up she stepped over three crushed tampons that had been trampled on. She assumed they probably fell out of someone's Louis Vuitton.

"Oh my God, Kristen, how did you ever come up with the plan to give the new girl fake directions? You must be really clever. Oh, wait, I'm sorry. Massie probably gave you the idea. I forgot you don't come up with anything on your own, do you?" Claire mumbled under her breath. She stomped up the stairs and straight down the hall, back to where she started.

The infirmary smelled like rubbing alcohol despite the vase of fresh pink roses on the reception desk.

"Hello, dear, how can I help you?" the nurse asked. Her voice was soothing and buttery.

"I need to see the nurse." Claire's eyes welled up with tears when she heard herself say those words. The morning's events had really taken a toll on her.

"I'm the nurse. My name's Adele." She lifted her index finger to the name embroidered on her lab coat.

Adele had shoulder-length auburn hair and soft green eyes. She looked kind and comforting, the way movie moms do in warm fuzzy flashback scenes.

"Have a seat and tell me what hurts."

"I'm fine. Honestly. I don't even know why I'm here." Claire tried to force a smile. "Vincent told me to come, but he wouldn't say why."

"Claire, would you mind standing up for me?" She spoke with confidence, like a detective who was seconds away from cracking a case.

Claire stood up carefully.

"Yup, just as I thought, you got your period," Adele said.

"No, I didn't!" Claire insisted.

"Look at the back of your jeans." Adele opened her desk, pulled out a large hand mirror, and passed it to Claire.

"No way!"

"It's perfectly natural, nothing at all to be embarrassed about. I'll get you some pamphlets about menstruation and a pair of new jeans from the lost and found," Adele said. "Be right back."

Claire knew this was impossible. She didn't even have boobs yet. There was no way she'd gotten her period. She rubbed her index finger along the red stain on her pants and realized that it was paint. She rewound her brain and paused on Alicia bumping into her during art. *Wow,* she thought, *what Massie wants, Massie gets.* And then the whole scene played back in front of her, and she was so embarrassed she couldn't even think straight.

Adele burst through the door pushing a wardrobe rack full of designer clothes.

"This is our lost and found. Don't worry, everything has been dry-cleaned," she said. "Go through and pick out something you like."

"Seriously?" Claire asked.

"Yeah, why not? The girls at this school *hardly* go looking for last year's clothes."

"Really?" Claire's blue eyes widened. "I would have to save for years to afford just one of the things on the rack."

"Take as much as you want." Adele smiled. "Getting your period is something to celebrate."

Claire could feel Adele watching her while she sifted through the Seven jeans, silk print blouses, rhinestone-speckled T-shirts, denim skirts, satin camisoles, cashmere sweaters, suede blazers, and leather pants.

"Are you new here, Claire?" Adele asked.

"It's that obvious, huh?"

"A little," Adele said. "But in a good way."

Claire wasn't sure exactly what she meant by that but

was grateful for the compliment. She was more than ready for a little kindness.

Claire thanked the nurse with a hug and promised to come back for a visit.

When Claire walked out of the nurse's office, she looked like she belonged at OCD. She was wearing a camel-colored cashmere tank top, dark denim flair jeans, and a pair of pointy Steve Madden boots. She felt bad for tossing her favorite white Gap jeans, but they were ruined anyway.

She walked straight to the café, with her toes squished and her head held high.

Massie waited for her friends to be seated and organized before she told them her good news. She sat patiently while (1) Dylan pulled the thick foil off her Zone lunch and sniffed the pale grilled chicken breast; (2) Alicia bit off the corners of several mustard packets and squirted them onto her veggie burger (no bun); and (3) Kristen dipped a banana into a styrofoam cup of fro yo.

When they were ready to focus, Massie leaned forward on her elbows and assumed the "gossip position." The others pushed their lunches to the side and followed.

Once their huddle was complete, Massie spoke.

"I'm looking at a minimum of twenty points for what I'm about to say," Massie said.

"What?" they all replied.

"I have plans with a Briarwood boy on Saturday," she said. Their faces lit up and she knew it no longer mattered that she hadn't been on the Labor Day shopping trip. She was still their hero.

"Why didn't you tell us in the car?" Alicia asked.

"'Cause I didn't want Claire to hear." Massie lifted her head out of the circle and scanned the room.

"When did you meet him?" Kristen asked.

"Yesterday, at Galwaugh Farms," Massie said.

"While you were *sick?*" Alicia asked.

"I wasn't sick all day," Massie said.

"Oh," Alicia said.

"I got a lot better." Massie gathered her hair and twisted it in a bun on the back of her head, then took the chopsticks that came with her spicy tuna rolls and slid them through the knot to keep everything in place. Then she continued.

"He is fifteen, ah-dorable, and has his own horse," Massie said.

"He sounds perfect," Kristen gushed. "He could be the *one.*"

"Tell us everything." Alicia nodded. "Every last little detail."

And she did.

Even though Claire had zero appetite, she slid an orange plastic tray along the silver rails in front of the food displays. It was the only way she could blend in while she evaluated the lunchtime scene. She passed sushi platters, tofu steaks, crudités, and a colorful "design your own salad" section, but she didn't care about any of it. She was too busy checking out the other girls. She didn't have to have grown up in Westchester to know that the table where she chose to sit in the next few minutes would brand her for life.

"Will that be all?" the checkout lady asked.

A girl in line behind Claire let out a chuckle.

Claire looked down at her tray and realized it was still empty. She reached into the box by the register and pulled out a Toblerone bar.

"Finally, a girl around here who actually eats chocolate," the checkout lady said. "How refreshing."

Claire smiled and wondered if it was really possible to be in a school where no one ate junk food.

But it was. Bottles of Glaceau water were on every table. Even if Claire *wanted* to order a bottle for herself, she wouldn't have known how to pronounce it. She tried to see what Massie was eating but couldn't get a good look.

She was in the far corner of the room with Alicia, Dylan, and Kristen. It was the only four-top in the café. All of the other tables were designed to fit at least six. The four girls were sitting with their heads close together, and Claire figured they were telling secrets. Every few seconds a laugh would erupt from the table and one of them would break free from the huddle just long enough to have a quick look around, to make sure they hadn't been overheard. The other girls in the cafeteria seemed to be overwhelmingly drawn to them. In a matter of only five minutes at least four different wannabes approached their table, each of their faces bright with an eager smile. Each girl stayed for a few minutes, but the second she walked away, Alicia, Dylan, Kristen, and Massie would go back to talking and giggling, probably about whoever had just stopped by for a chat.

Claire knew a seat at that table would guarantee her a promising future at OCD, but considering the morning she had just had, she refused to let herself fantasize about it. It was never going to happen.

Not every table seemed as exclusive as Massie's, but they didn't seem as appealing either. One group of heavily painted girls looked like someone on the Psychic Friends Network did their makeup. And another group was so thin, they looked like the lipstick-covered straws that floated inside their diet Coke cans. Three girls, who Claire assumed were wrestlers because their necks and shoulders touched, pounded cartons of milk by the table next to the bathroom. She considered taking their picture and calling it "Got Friends?" but she was hardly one to talk.

A white flash of light that came from one of the middle tables suddenly caught her attention. It was followed by loud bursts of laughter that filled the café. Claire made these girls her target. She watched as everyone tried to distance themselves from the hysterics by pulling their chairs in closer to their tables or by walking away before they had finished eating. Claire thought about going over to these laughing girls and trying to sit with them. Would this be a good move, politically? Maybe not. But at least she'd finally have a little fun.

Claire reached in the cell phone pocket of her backpack (which held makeup and gum because a phone was out of the question until she turned sixteen) and pulled out her grape-scented lip gloss. She applied two coats and then dipped the wand back in its tube.

"Excuse me." Claire was standing behind two of the girls and facing another. "Is that a PowerShot S100 digital Elph?"

Three faces turned toward Claire at the exact same time. They were still smiling from whatever had happened before Claire interrupted them.

"Yeah, I just got it for my birthday," the photographer said. Her hair was separated into seven braids. She wore faded jeans with suspenders and a pink tank top.

"That's so funny, I have the exact same one." Claire searched through her bag, looking for the proof. "I take it everywhere." She held the tiny silver camera in the palm of her hand as if it were a baby bird.

The other girls at the table had rhinestone tattoos on

their upper arms. One had a blue butterfly and the other a pink heart.

"Are those real?" Claire pointed to the rhinestones and smiled. She wanted the girls to know she was joking. But it didn't work.

"No," the girl with the butterfly said. "We got them from the drugstore for like a buck twenty."

"Oh, well, around here you never know," Claire said. "I wouldn't be surprised if those Picassos on the wall were real." She pointed to the paintings that hung inside glass cases around the room.

"They are," said the girl with the pink heart.

The girl with the butterfly wore red cords and a T-shirt with the devil on it that said, DADDY'S LITTLE GIRL. The one with the heart was dressed in blue-and-white-striped jeans, like the kind train conductors wear, and a black I ♥ CARBS T-shirt. They both had yellow, green, and orange streaks, which Claire knew was hair mascara, because a lot of the girls in her old school had been into it.

Claire could feel Massie's eyes on her from all the way across the room. She did her best to ignore the icy glares and tried to look like she was making friends.

"What were you guys laughing about?" Claire asked.

The girl looked at her friends to see if they thought if was safe before she continued.

"Do you have Vincent for art?" she asked.

"Yeah."

"Well, we're taking pictures of ourselves acting out his

different expressions," the girl said. She pushed a button on the back of the camera and shuttled through the images she had already shot. She held the camera out in front of Claire so she could see the screen from the other side of the table. "Here's Meena acting out 'you're tardy!' and this is one of Heather 'in love with a vase of flowers.'"

Claire started laughing.

"Do you want to try?" the girl asked. "Okay, show me *lost.*"

Claire put what was left of her fingernails in her mouth and forced the corners of her lips toward her chin. This made the veins on her neck stick out. She opened her eyes as wide as they would go and slid both of her pupils to the right as if she'd just heard a frightening sound.

The flash went off and the girls exploded. The one with the FCUK T-shirt laughed so hard a little milk dribbled out her nose.

Claire checked to see if Massie was still watching her. She was.

"My name is Layne," the girl with the camera offered. Claire thought the girl looked like a female version of Tom Cruise, with her big nose, green eyes, and slightly crooked smile. The wild braided hair seemed to be the only thing keeping her from a career as his stunt double.

"This is Heather and Meena," Layne said.

"Hi." Heather smiled.

"Hi." Meena smiled too.

"I'm Claire."

"Aren't you Massie's friend?" Heather asked.

Before Claire answered, she checked to make sure Massie wasn't watching her anymore.

"Uh, yeah, I am," Claire said softly. "How'd you know?"

"I saw you with her this morning. And you're dressed like a pure Massie-chist."

Claire was glad she wasn't in the clothes she'd worn school that day or they never would have believed her.

"Um, since I'm new here, I'm trying to meet everyone," Claire said. "Massie was bummed about it at first because she was scared I'd make other friends and dump her—"

"She *told* you that?" Layne asked.

"Not exactly." Claire bit her lip. "She wrote it in an e-mail."

"*No* way," Meena said. "What did she write?"

Heather looked at her watch and let out a loud whine. "Meena, we have to meet LuLu about getting into her dressmaking class," she said.

"I can't believe we have to leave right when the Massie gossip is getting started," Meena said.

"Don't worry, I have plenty more Massie stories. I'll tell you everything next time," Claire said.

"Promise?" Meena asked.

"Promise." Claire raised her palm in the air like she was being sworn in under oath. Okay, so it wasn't really true. But better to be a liar than a loser, right?

Now that the girls were gone, Claire realized she had been standing up that whole time. She felt awkward looking down at Layne, who was seated.

"Did you eat yet?" Layne asked. "'Cause I have tons of

oatmeal left if you want some—it's protein enriched. I bring it every day from home. I'm addicted."

Claire appreciated the offer, but the thought of sharing goopy oatmeal from a stranger's thermos made her want to dry-heave.

"No, thanks," Claire lied.

She was talking to Layne but kept her eyes fixed on Massie, who sat down at a nearby table to talk to some friends. Claire shifted in her seat uncomfortably and only half paid attention to her conversation with Layne.

After a very short visit Claire watched Massie program some girls' numbers into her cell phone. Alicia, Dylan, and Kristen turned three-quarters and waved goodbye from over their shoulders. Claire seemed to be the next stop on their table tour, because they were walking straight toward her.

Wild geese that fly with the moon on their wings
These are a few of my favorite things. . . .

Claire caught a whiff of Massie's perfume and knew they were getting closer. Before she could decide if she should get up and run or hide under the table, the four girls had arrived. Layne looked at Claire to see how she would greet them, probably hoping for an introduction. But nothing happened. They brushed by the table and didn't say a word to anyone.

False alarm.

"Jeez," Layne said. "Massie is *really* jealous."

"I told you." Claire ran her fingers across her bangs, suddenly anxious about how they looked. But the second Massie left the café, Claire relaxed.

Layne and Claire spent the rest of lunch period talking about their mutual love of old musicals (especially *Sound of Music, Annie,* and *Wizard of Oz*), skater boys, and digital cameras. They hated the snobby factor of *Teen Vogue* and thought Drew Barrymore seemed like she'd be kinda bitchy.

"We are such soul sisters," Claire said.

"I know," Layne said. "We have to start hanging out." She wiped a glob off the side of her thermos and packed it up in her backpack

Claire, suddenly embarrassed for Layne, scrambled to focus on something else.

"That is the coolest bag I've ever seen," Claire said.

It had a dark green shell that opened like the trunk on a scooter. The surface was covered in stickers from different snowboard companies, except for two spots on the either side. That's where the stereo speakers were.

Layne pushed a button on the top of the bag and a techno remix blasted through the room.

The diet Coke girls whipped their heads around to find the source of the sudden noise. Once they saw Layne holding her bag up to her ear, they lost interest and turned back to their sodas.

"It has a CD player built into it. I got it for fifty bucks. Can you believe?" Layne said.

"Half the bags I've seen around here cost ten times more and *they* don't do *anything!*" Claire exclaimed.

Layne laughed.

"Hey, Friday night, wanna go to a movie or listen to my bag or something?" she asked.

"Yeah, I would love to." Claire hugged her new friend and gave her a huge smile, but deep down inside, a little nagging part of her wished she had been invited to sit at an A-list table instead.

"Maybe I should check with my mom first," Claire said.

The heavy oak doors of Briarwood Academy flew open and a rush of boys in gray jackets and red ties poured out of the building and stomped all over the grass in the middle of the huge circular driveway. Massie, Alicia, and Dylan were hiding across the street from the boys' school, but thanks to the binoculars they'd "borrowed" from the science lab, they felt like they could touch it.

"Shhhhhh, here they come," Massie whispered. She ducked behind the manicured row of hedges where Alicia and Dylan were already crouched and in position.

Dylan let the binoculars dangle from the string around her neck so she could tear the stubborn silver foil off her Zone bar. To Massie, the crinkling wrapper sounded like nickels raining down on a tin roof.

"*Shhhhhh,*" Massie whispered again.

"It's not like he can hear me from all the way—," Dylan started. But Massie quickly put her hand over Dylan's mouth to shut her up.

"I don't see him," Alicia whispered. "What does he look like again?"

"Leo DiCaprio, before he got doughy," Massie said.

"Every guy here looks like that," Alicia said.

"Yeah, but Chris Abeley has messy hair—in blond!" Massie said.

Like most hot guys, Chris Abeley was a "firsty-lasty." This meant no one called him "Chris" and no one called him "Abeley." He was always Chris Abeley.

"Mmmmerrrrrrr." Dylan tried to speak, but Massie's hand was still in the way. After two silent minutes Dylan forced her tongue through her smashed lips and licked Massie's palm.

"Ew!" Massie quickly removed her hand.

Dylan took a huge bite of her chocolate raspberry supreme bar and wagged her food-filled tongue at Massie.

"You're disgusting." Massie laughed. She wiped her hand across the hedges to dry it off.

"What would you rather?" Alicia asked with a mischievous smile. "A kiss from Chris Abeley after he ate a bag of Cool Ranch Doritos and drank pickle juice or . . . a kiss from Chris Abeley after he barfed up clam chowder?"

"Both," Massie said. "Now be quiet!"

The stakeout had required a lot of preparation. First Massie had to tell Isaac that she was going to the library after school and that he wouldn't need to pick her up until 4:30 P.M.. Once the pickup was confirmed, she had to plan their escape from OCD. Since both schools let out at the exact same time and were precisely seven minutes apart, they had to be on the move no later than 3:13 P.M. Massie would have been fine with 3:14 if they had been wearing comfortable shoes, but they weren't. Everyone had made it as planned except Kristen, who had yet to show.

"I think I see him, over there at three o'clock. Beside the statue of that army guy," Dylan said.

"No, there's a prefat Leo by the bike rack," Alicia said. She was pointing straight ahead.

"That's not him. There are prefat Leos all over the place—look for the messy hair," Massie said.

"So he really asked you to meet him on Saturday?" Alicia asked. She was looking through her binoculars while she spoke.

"He said, and I quote, I'll be back next Saturday when the trails are open to the public. Maybe I'll see you then? End quote. Then he said, and I quote, It's a date. End quote," Massie said.

"Was he making eye contact with you when he said, 'It's a date'?" Dylan asked.

"Full on. He even winked." Massie let her binoculars fall around her neck and looked at her friends. "A *wink*."

Alicia and Kristen dropped their gear and slowly turned to face Massie. It was as if she had just told them she was engaged to be married.

"That's sooooo amazing!" Alicia squealed.

All three girls hugged each other and started bouncing up and down.

"This looks more like a freak-out than a stakeout." Kristen stood in front of them with a serious look on her face and waited for an explanation. "What did I miss?" She was struggling to untangle the knots in the rope that hung from her binoculars.

"Nothing, we were just talking about Chris Abeley," Dylan said.

"Again?" Kristen said.

"Where were you?" Massie asked.

"We ended up getting this major assignment in Women in the Workforce and I couldn't just leave," Kristen said.

"Shhh," Massie said.

"What do you have to do?" Alicia whispered.

"I have to start my own company," Kristen practically mouthed. "The whole walk here I was trying to come up with an idea and I couldn't think of anything."

Alicia picked up her binoculars and wiped the lenses off on the inside of her blazer. She had already lost interest.

"Maybe you should invent something for people who don't have ideas," Dylan said.

Massie and Alicia laughed.

"How 'bout something for people who make really *stupid* suggestions," Kristen snapped back.

"How 'bout something that helps me find Chris Abeley," Massie suggested sarcastically.

Everyone returned to their posts.

"Are you sure we didn't miss him already?" Kristen asked.

"Yeah, I'm sure."

"How do you know?" Kristen asked.

"Because I'm looking right at him," Massie said slowly, as if any sudden movement would blow her cover.

"Ehmagod, where?" Alicia asked.

But they spotted him before Massie had a chance to tell them. He was the only person walking down the front steps of the building. Massie wasn't sure if everyone on the campus had suddenly vanished or if it just felt that way because she only had eyes for him. He had a beat-up leather book bag over his shoulder and a can of Red Bull.

"*Oh.*"

"*My.*"

"*God.*"

"Zoom in as tight as you can," Massie said. "See that freckle right above his lip? How hot is that?"

Massie pulled a tube of gloss out of her denim blazer and managed to apply it without putting down her binoculars.

"It looks like he's walking toward us, doesn't it?" Kristen said.

"Yeah, almost like he knows Massie's here," Dylan offered. "Could this be any more romantic?" Dylan spit a pit out of her mouth after she spoke. She reached into a Ziploc bag and pulled out another cherry. Her red-stained lips were the only proof that the bag had been full minutes ago.

"*Shhh.* He's crossing the street," Massie said.

Chris Abeley walked directly over to the hedge that separated him from the girls. He stood with his back facing them. Inches away the four girls were having a frantic conversation, using only their wide, panic-filled eyes to communicate.

Kristen reached out her hand and pretended to squeeze

Chris Abeley's butt. This made Alicia and Dylan shake with suppressed laughter. Even Massie had to fight the urge to crack up.

MASSIE: WHAT IZY W8ing 4?
DYLAN: U
MASSIE: ☺

Massie was enjoying the thought of Chris Abeley waiting for her after school too much to notice that something cool and sticky was trickling down her back. She lifted her head slowly. A stream of pink liquid was making its way from a can of Red Bull onto her scalp. Massie covered her phone with both hands to protect it from the moisture.

A blue BMW blasting tinny guitar-heavy boy music pulled up in front of Chris Abeley.

"How was detention?" a guy's voice shouted over the music.

"Killer!" Chris Abeley cheered sarcastically. "Best time ever."

He scooped his bag off the ground and whipped the empty can behind the hedge. It ricocheted off Alicia's kneecap and she let out a loud yelp. Luckily the drum solo that blasted from the car's stereo kept her from being heard.

As soon as the car sped off, the girls rolled around on the grass howling with laughter. They held their stomachs and wiped the tears from their eyes as they pointed at Massie's wet hair. Once they finally caught their breath,

Alicia's bright red knee made them crack up all over again.

"You guys look ridiculous," Dylan said.

"Look who's talking." Alicia pointed at the mountain of cherry pits piled high beside Dylan.

Her lips were so red, she looked like the Joker from *Batman*.

"You know, that's not a bad color," Massie said. "I wish someone sold that."

Dylan pulled her silver hairbrush out of her bag and flipped it over.

"You're right." Dylan puckered up for her reflection and blew herself a kiss.

"Maybe she's born with it," Massie sang.

"Maybe its Maybelline," the others responded.

Later that night, before she went to sleep, Massie made a record of the afternoon's events.

CURRENT STATE OF THE UNION	
IN	**OUT**
RIDING	HIDING
RED CHERRIES	RED BULL

Massie and Dylan stared at themselves in the bathroom mirrors while they spoke.

"I can't believe my lips are still stained." Dylan grabbed a soft white facial towel off the cosmetics table by the window and rubbed it across her lips, but it only made them look redder.

"Top it off with a clear gloss and you'd be onto something," Massie said to Dylan's reflection.

"It's not funny. My sisters called me Liperacchi all night and my mother threatened to cancel my Zone deliveries if I keep eating high-sugar fruits that aren't part of the program," Dylan said.

Massie slid a tube of gold shimmer across her lips.

"I wish my makeup lasted that long," she said.

"Maybe Kristen should start a makeup company for her class project," Dylan joked. "She can sell cherries."

"Brilliant!" Massie clapped with excitement. "We'll make everything ourselves using all-natural ingredients. Your mom can have us on *The Daily Grind* so we can promote our new line and—"

"Are you kidding?" Dylan asked. "Do you really think it's a good idea or are you just making fun of me?" Dylan worked her brush through a tangle.

"No, I'm serious," Massie said.

"We'll call it Homebody," Dylan suggested. "You know, because all of our 'body' products will be made from 'home.'" She added air quotes to "home" and "body" just in case Massie didn't get how genius her suggestion was.

"Maybe the name should be more glamorous," Massie said.

Dylan pulled strands of red hair out of her brush and shook them to the ground, but they clung to her like spiderwebs.

"I think it's all about being catchy and clever," Dylan pushed.

"There's nothing catchy or clever about Guerlain, Dior, or Clarins," Massie said. "And they're doing a little better than Hard Candy and Urban Decay, don't you think?"

"Maybe this whole thing is stupid," Dylan said. "We have no clue how to make cosmetics."

"That's what the Internet is for," Massie said.

"Do you think Kristen will like it?" Dylan asked.

"We'll *make* her like it." Massie walked into a bathroom stall and closed the door behind her. The discussion was over.

"You can go ahead without me—I may be a while," Massie offered.

"'Kay," Dylan answered.

"We're gonna be rich!" Massie sang. Her swinging feet were visible through the opening at the bottom of the stall.

"We already are," Dylan said on her way out. "See ya at lunch, Coco."

"Au revoir, Estee," Massie said.

When Massie was sure Dylan was gone, she reached into her bag and pulled out her PalmPilot. She was feeling inspired. She thought about how great it would be to have everyone in the school, especially the older girls, rely on her for the latest beauty products and makeup advice. Chris Abeley would be in awe of her high-powered hobby and forget all about their age difference. She would never have to worry about little things like Claire threatening her social status again. She would be untouchable.

CURRENT STATE OF THE UNION	
IN	**OUT**
HOMEBODY	BODY SHOP
CEOs	BFFs
MAKEUP MOGUL	FASHION DESIGNER

"Did Mom tell you I'm having a sleepover party tonight?" Todd asked Claire. She was lying on the white L-shaped couch, flipping through the TV channels and eating mint chocolate-chip ice cream.

Claire rolled her eyes. "I'm going out with my new friend Layne," she said.

Todd reached over and tried to force his spoon into the carton, but Claire blocked him with her elbow.

"Wait, how many people are coming over?" Claire asked. She found it hard to believe he already knew enough people invite to a "party."

"Eleven," Todd said. "Twelve if Stevie Levine can get out of his stepbrother's bar mitzvah dinner."

Todd lunged again, knocked Claire's spoon out of the way, and scooped out the biggest chunk of chocolate there was. Claire didn't flinch.

"How do you have twelve friends already?" Claire asked.

"The raisins." Todd said. "I told you."

Kendra knocked lightly on the front door, letting herself in before anyone could answer. She was wearing a pair of crisp-looking black pants and a baby blue cashmere sweater set. Even when she was just spending the day at home, she still looked perfectly put together.

As soon as Claire spotted Kendra she took her feet off the couch and sat up straight.

"My mom isn't home," Claire said.

"Actually, I came to see you, Claire." Kendra's voice was calm and smooth.

"Oh!" Claire squeaked with surprise. "You did?"

"Every Friday night Massie has a sleepover and I'd like you to come tonight," Kendra said. "That is, of course, if you don't already have plans."

"Thanks, but I'm sure Massie doesn't want me at her party," Claire said.

"Who would?" Todd said.

"Shut up," Claire mumbled. She pinched her brother on the arm and kicked him off the couch. None of this fazed Kendra. She was all business.

"I insist," Kendra said. "And Massie insists. Come by at 7:30 P.M. and don't worry about a sleeping bag; we'll have everything you need."

"*Massie* insists?" Claire asked.

"Yes."

"Okay," Claire said. "Thanks."

"Wait, I thought you already had pla—," Todd tried to say. But Claire kicked him off the couch again before he could finish.

The instant Claire heard the front door close, she jumped off the couch and ran upstairs to her bedroom.

She grabbed a jumble of clothes off the chair in front of her desk, tossed them onto the floor, and sat down at her computer. As soon as she moved the mouse, her dancing bananas screen saver melted away, revealing her wallpaper—a picture of her friends back home. In the picture Sarah, Sari, and Mandy were sitting in a speedboat waving at the camera. Their cheeks were all squished because their life jackets were too tight, and their hair was matted down with spray. They had their arms around each other and they were smiling big, goofy smiles. Just looking at that picture made Claire's chest feel tight. She hadn't called them since school started because she was scared she'd cry when she heard their voices. She was about to IM them and ask how she should cancel her plans with Layne, but she knew they'd just tell her not to. They'd tell her to forget about Massie and her snobby friends, and Claire didn't feel like explaining why she couldn't. Shame forced her to come up with an excuse all on her own.

Claire started looking around for Layne's number.

"I know, Layne, it totally sucks," Claire said into the white cordless phone. "*Especially* on a Friday night." She paced back and forth in her bedroom, stepping lightly to avoid the creaking hardwood floors.

"I'd be happy to come over and help you babysit if you want," Layne offered.

"Uh, that's probably not such a good idea." Claire rubbed her nose. "Todd is really sick and highly contagious."

"Bummer."

Claire paced again. She couldn't tell if Layne knew she was lying.

"Can we do something tomorrow?" Claire asked.

"Sure, around noon?"

"Perfect," Claire said. "Thanks for being so understanding."

"No big," Layne said. And then Layne started to say something else, but Claire didn't hear a word of it.

Claire was so nervous, she'd already hung up.

Claire arrived at the sleepover half an hour late because she didn't want to seem anxious. By the time she got there, everyone else was already in the living room, dancing on the brown leather couches. Claire could see them through the big picture window, but when she knocked on the side door, no one answered. She figured they couldn't hear her. The music was probably up too loud, she reasoned.

So Claire opened the door a crack and poked her head in. "Hello," she called. "Hello?" The house smelled warm and sweet, like chocolate chip cookies.

"In here, Claire," Kendra called back.

Claire walked into the living room and instantly felt her muscles tense. She was wearing her favorite blue-and-white sheep print pajamas. Massie, Dylan, Alicia and Kristen were fully dressed.

Pop music blasted from the speakers that hung in every corner and a giant glass bowl of popcorn was sitting on the glass coffee table. Heaps of clothes were spread all across the floor.

"All right, girls," Kendra said, lowering the volume on the stereo. "The break is over. I need help packing this stuff up."

Kendra began picking pieces of clothing up off the floor one by one—dark denim jeans, candy-colored sweaters, wool coats, nylon jackets, designer print T-shirts, stretchy skirts, and knit doggie clothes. She'd hold each one out in front of her for a brief second and then quickly fold it into a crisp rectangle and place it neatly in one of the many cardboard boxes that sat on the floor. The other girls were halfheartedly doing the same. Claire was hypnotized. No one acknowledged her except for Bean, who ran up to her and sniffed her toes.

"Hi, Bean." Claire crouched down to pat the dog.

Before Claire was able to make contact, Massie let out a high-pitched whistle and Bean scampered back to her mistress.

"Claire, we're so glad you could come," Kendra said.

Massie glanced up. "Nice jammies," she said. Then she went back to folding.

Not one of the other girls even looked her way.

"Why are you getting rid of *that?*" Massie asked Dylan. "You just bought it on Labor Day."

"It makes me look fat!" Dylan held the thick white cashmere sweater in her arms so she could see it from a distance. The price tag dangled off the sleeve. "What was I thinking, buying white?"

"Lemme see, maybe I'll take it," Kristen said.

She held the sweater beside her face, but the girls shook their heads no.

"Into the box it goes," Kristen said. She bit off the $300 price tag and handed the sweater to Kendra.

"What are you guys doing?" Claire finally asked.

No one said a word until Kendra cleared her throat in

a very loud you-better-say-something-*now* sort of way.

"We host an auction here every year to raise money for OCD scholarships," Massie said.

"Looks like you're getting rid of a lot," Claire said.

"Well, of course we are. All of this is *last* season," Alicia said. "After we're done, we go on a shopping spree to replace it all with brand-new stuff."

Claire felt a rush of panic rip through her body. The kind she'd felt when she waved back to Andy Jeffries (her sixth-grade crush) before she realized he was waving at Becky Manning. It was the same general feeling of cluelessness. She had been wearing the same pair of Gap jeans for a year and a half, up until the paint incident.

No one had told her clothes were like milk or cheese, with a "best before" date and a shelf life. The only time she ever threw anything out was when it got stained or if she grew out of it.

"I have a bunch of stuff I can donate," Claire offered.

"*No!*" the four girls said in unison.

Claire cocked her head and scrunched her eyebrows.

"The whole idea of the auction is to *make* money." Alicia rolled her eyes.

"I know *that*," Claire said. "I'll go get some things and I'll be right back."

"I don't understand why it's such a big deal to you," Massie said to her mother. They were standing in the kitchen pantry surrounded by cans of soup, bottles of mineral water, bags of pretzels, and boxes of doggie biscuits, which Bean was sniffing. For some reason this was always the place her mother chose to talk when Massie was about to be in trouble for something.

"She is a guest in our house, not to mention a very lovely girl. I know you'll really like her if you give her a chance," Kendra said. One of her hands rested on the thick wood countertop and the other was on her tiny waist. She was wearing a black Juicy sweat suit and a pearl choker.

"Mom, why don't you stop worrying about *her* so much and start thinking about how all of your matchmaking is affecting me!" Massie said. Her voice shook as she spoke and she was scared if she said any more, she would start to cry. "It's like you care about her happiness more than you care about mine!"

Massie stormed out of the pantry and locked herself in the yellow-and-white downstairs bathroom. She sprayed some French rosewater on her face and gently dabbed it dry with a fluffy yellow towel, making sure to pat, not rub. She'd once read in *Seventeen* that it was a crime against beauty to wipe your face with a towel because it pulled the skin and caused wrinkles.

"Mass," Kristen called through the door. "We're going out to the cabana to set up—you coming?"

Massie cleared her throat and forced her voice to sound normal. "Go ahead," she called back. "I'll see you guys out there in a bit."

Massie sat down on top of the closed toilet and read old issues of *Town and Country* for about ten minutes until she heard her mother go upstairs for the night. When she opened the door, Bean was right there waiting for her.

Massie was about to head outside to the cabana when she heard a noise coming from the living room. She slid off her flip-flops to avoid slapping noises and carried Bean in her arms so the tags and charms around her Gucci collar wouldn't clang. She figured Kristen had snuck back in to swipe a few things out of the box, just like she'd done the year before, and she wanted to catch her in the act.

Massie poked her head in the doorway of the living room. Ribbons of yellow light, sent from lampposts on the front lawn, broke up the darkness and helped Massie see the box. As soon as she spotted it, there all alone in the middle of the big room, a wave of loneliness filled the pit of her stomach. She got the same feeling around Christmas when she'd look at the tree in the middle of the night. Something about seeing it all tall and proud, decorated with lights and surrounded by presents, seemed so depressing. Like looking at someone who was all dressed up with nowhere to go. Massie heard something brush up against the cardboard. She leaned in to get a closer look. It was Claire. She was kneeling beside the box and feeding it folded sweatshirts. She had a soft semismile on her face. She looked both peaceful and proud.

"At least they both have company," Massie whispered into Bean's batlike ear. She gave Bean a squeeze and slowly crept away.

┌─────────────────────────────────────┐
│   │
│   THE BLOCK ESTATE   │
│   CABANA #3   │
│   10:15 P.M.   │
│   September 5th   │
│   │
└─────────────────────────────────────┘

"Sorry I took so long." Massie shut off her flashlight and put Bean on the floor. "I had to take her for a walk."

Four sleeping bags were laid out like the spokes of a bicycle wheel, and Bean's white sheepskin bed was in the center. A glass bowl filled with butter-flavored soy crisps and Junior Mints—the ultimate combo—was on Dylan's lap. They were in the middle of an intense round of What Would You Rather?

"'Kay, what would you rather?" Alicia asked. "A condition that makes you snore twenty-four seven or a condition that makes you fall down every ten seconds?"

"Snore," Dylan said.

"Snore," Kristen agreed.

"What would you rather have, a long curly pig's tail or Chihuahua ears sticking out of the top of your head?" Kristen asked.

"The tail would be like having one big panty line all the time, so I'm going with Chihuahua ears," Alicia said.

"Tail for me!" Dylan said. "I already look like a pig, so I might as well just go with it." She snorted and stuffed a handful of soy crisps and Junior Mints in her mouth.

"You do *not* look like a pig!" Kristen snapped.

"You just smell like one." Massie was trying to lighten

the mood. The *last* thing she needed right now was for the night to turn into yet another Dr. Phil session about Dylan and her insecurities.

"I have one," Massie offered. "What would you rather be? (*a*) Completely and utterly friendless or (*b*) someone with tons of friends who secretly hate you?"

The other girls were silently weighing their options, but Massie knew her answer right away. She would pick (*b*) no question—in both scenarios she'd have no friends, but at least in the second scenario she wouldn't be alone.

"I'd definitely pick friendless loser." Alicia flipped her hair. "I wouldn't want to live a lie."

"Same with me," Kristen agreed.

"Ditto," Dylan said. "What about you, Massie?"

"Friendless loser, of course." Massie added an eye roll for believability.

Claire walked into the cabana holding her CD case. Massie saw her examine the sleeping bag situation.

"What a great setup." Claire's cheeks were flushed from running to the different houses. "This is so much better than my brother's setup. You should see—" Claire stopped talking when she counted four sleeping bags instead of five.

Massie watched the tiny pulses beat like a heart on the side of Claire's jaw.

"Claire, what would *you* rather be?" Alicia asked. "A friendless loser or a person with tons of friends who secretly don't like you?"

"A person with tons of friends who secretly don't like me," she said quickly.

The other girls exchanged a look and Massie couldn't decide if she thought Claire's honesty was brave or stupid.

"Congratulations, you're halfway there. The 'friends' part is the only thing you're missing," Alicia tossed off coolly.

Alicia looked at Massie for approval because her comment was nasty times ten, but she got nothing. Massie's attention was on the zipper of her sleeping bag, which she was pretending to struggle with.

"I'm kidding, Claire," Alicia said. "It was a joke."

"Oh, is that what that was?" Claire's face was bright red, but her voice was calm. "Where I come from, jokes are funny."

Kristen laughed but was instantly silenced by Alicia's glare.

"Are there any more sleeping bags?" Claire asked, turning toward Massie. "Your mom said you had extras."

"In the closet by the bathroom," Massie said. Everyone sat there for a second, not moving.

"Guess what I have?" Dylan broke the silence. She waved a piece of paper around in the air. "Cute coma guy's phone number."

"NO way, let me call." Alicia pulled the paper out of Dylan's hands and the girls gathered around Alicia so they could all listen in. "I can't believe I'm about to talk to the hottest guy on *Young and the Restless*," Alicia whispered to her friends.

"Hello?" a guy's voice answered.

"It's *him*," Alicia mouthed. "Uh, yeah, this is May, your dead wife. I know what you and Melanie did and as soon as you come out of that coma, I will haunt you for the rest of your life." The girls laughed so hard they shook.

Massie snuck a peek at Claire, who was setting up her sleeping bag outside the circle.

Another man's voice got on the line. "Honey, who is it?" he asked.

Alicia slammed the phone down and shouted, "Oh my gawd, cute coma guy is gay!"

"Someone should tell his mistress, Melanie, that her boy isn't who she thinks he is," Kristen said.

"Speaking of boys, I can't believe you're going riding at Galwaugh Farms with Chris Abeley tomorrow." Dylan rolled over on her sleeping bag so she was lying on her stomach. Her knees were bent and her chin was propped up on her hands. The other girls assumed the same position so all of their heads faced each other.

"What are you going to wear?" Kristen asked.

"I don't know. I haven't really thought about it," Massie said.

Claire was tempted to shout, "Puh-lease! I've watched you try on outfits all week from my bedroom window."

But she didn't.

"What if he tries to kiss you?" Dylan asked. "He *is* fifteen, you know."

"Then I'll kiss him back." Massie smeared a glob of lip

gloss on her lips like a cunning soap opera seductress and attacked her pillow.

*Ewwwww*s and laughter filled the room.

Massie lifted her head out of the pillow and smoothed her disheveled hair.

"A few cherries to rub on your lips and you'll be good to go." Dylan looked at Kristen with her hands clasped together like she was a starving beggar.

"Will you guys stop bugging me about this homemade cosmetics company thing?" Kristen said. "You've been driving me crazy."

"Yeah, Dylan, maybe the idea of being rich and powerful isn't Kristen's thing," Massie said.

"Right now all I'm interested in is an A," Kristen said. She looked at her friends' pleading faces and let out a heavy sigh. "Let's just say I agreed—what would we call it?"

"What about Homebody?" Dylan said. "It'd be, y'know, ironic. Because people would wear it when they were going out."

"I think it should be something more glamorous," Massie said. "Don't you, Kristen?"

Dylan rolled her eyes and took tiny squirrel-size bites out of the last soy chip.

"I totally agree," Kristen nodded.

"What about Shimmer Down?" Claire asked.

No one responded.

"I've got it," Massie announced. "Glambition!"

"I love it." Kristen smiled.

"Me too," Alicia added.

Dylan and Claire were silent.

"Let's do it." Kristen lifted her bottle of Perrier and the rest of the girls did the same.

"To Glambition!" They clinked their bottles and gulped their lemon-lime seltzers. The fizz burned against their throats and they all let out big *ahhhhh*s when they finished swallowing.

Then everyone changed into their pajamas, except for Alicia, who stayed in her T-shirt and bra. They started settling into their sleeping bags.

"Does anyone want to hear a ghost story?" Claire asked from across the room.

"Sure," Massie said before the other girls could protest.

"Can I borrow that flashlight?" Claire asked Massie.

"Yep," Massie said. "I'll get it."

She was a little more agreeable than usual and Claire couldn't help wondering why.

"Can we turn off all the lights?" Claire asked.

"Allow me," Massie said with a half smile.

Once the room was pitch black, Claire positioned the flashlight under her chin and turned it on.

"The red reflection from the flashlight makes you look like Satan," Alicia said.

"I am Satan," Claire growled in a slow scary whisper. "Now I want you all to lie down."

"Yes, teacher," Kristen sing-songed.

Giggles broke out.

"Okay. Ready?" she asked without expecting an answer.

"A guy is driving to the movies with his girlfriend one night and it starts to thunder. Suddenly a flash of lightning strikes and the streetlights go out. . . . It's a total blackout." Claire paused for dramatic effect before continuing. "They decide to pull over to the side of the empty highway to wait until the storm lightens up a bit. They start making out because there's really nothing else for them to do, when suddenly the car radio comes on by itself and—"

Claire was cut off by Alicia, who sneezed the word *boring*.

"ZZZZzzzzzzzzzzzz." Dylan made a snoring noise.

"Mi mi mi mi mi mi mi mi miiiiii," Kristen joined in.

By this point Alicia, Dylan, Kristen, and Massie were in complete hysterics and Claire was lying on her back staring at the ceiling fan.

Eventually the laughter died down and a hush fell over the room.

"I'm tired," Dylan said. And then everyone was silent.

Massie hated this part of sleepovers, the winding down. She hated being the last one awake, so usually she would ask one of the girls a question that required a really long answer and while they were talking, she would try to fall asleep. But before Massie had a chance, Alicia broke the silence by making a loud fart noise with her mouth.

"Claire!" she said. "Was that you?"

The girls laughed, but in a tired, lazy way.

"Actually, Alicia, I thought it was your boobs rubbing together," Claire said.

Massie buried her face in the pillow so no one would hear her laugh.

"I wish it was your thighs rubbing together on your way back to O-Town," Alicia snapped.

After that no one said anything. Massie couldn't tell if everyone had fallen asleep or if they were just pretending.

She held her breath for a second so she could listen for any whimpering sounds that might be coming from Claire. But there weren't any.

Massie felt vaguely uneasy, and she knew sleep was out of the question. She pulled Bean close and thought of the first time she'd seen the dog in the pet store window. Bean was no bigger than a hamster, but she was in a cage with two golden retrievers and a Jack Russell terrier. Every time she went to play with one of the squeaky toys, the other dogs yapped at her so she would drop it. But Bean never did. Even when she got pounced on and clawed, she held on to the toy as hard as she could. That toy was what she wanted and she wasn't letting go. Massie admired that fighting quality in her dog, but at the same time it made her heart hurt in a way she couldn't quite figure out. She now found herself feeling the exact same thing about Claire.

Massie heard someone stirring. She closed her eyes three-quarters of the way so whoever it was wouldn't know she was awake.

It was Claire. She was rolling her sleeping bag up as quietly as she possibly could. After three rolls she'd pause, check to see that no was had woken up, and then she'd roll some more. Once she was packed up, she slipped out the front door.

Massie waited to make sure no one else was awake and then got up. "Where are you going?" Massie whispered. She stood in the doorway with Bean and watched Claire walk barefoot across the damp grass.

"I can't sleep—I'm going home." Claire paused. "I mean, I'm going to *your* guesthouse."

Massie looked over at her sleeping friends. She closed the door before speaking again.

"Why don't you stay? We were just joking around. We do it to everyone," Massie said.

"I'd just rather sleep on a mattress than a floor," Claire lied. Massie could hear that she was holding back tears.

"Well, if you've *got* to go, use my flashlight for the walk home," Massie said. "Hold on, I'll run inside and get it."

Massie walked back to the house, confused. It wasn't *her* fault if Claire had social problems. Right? So why did she suddenly feel a weird desire to help her?

Massie found the flashlight where Claire had been lying. She walked outside on the cold grass. "I found it," Massie whispered. But Bean's jingling collar was all she heard.

"Claire?" Massie said into the night air.

"Claire!"

The sound of her own voice echoed in her head and it

sounded creepy, like it didn't belong to her. Maybe because she'd said Claire's name with a trace of concern, maybe because it was the first time she'd called someone's name and gotten no response, or maybe because she felt like a Christmas tree, all alone in the dark, with no one to appreciate her.

"Excuse me," Claire said softly, "would you *mind* getting out of my bed?" She nudged the stranger with the dyed blue hair, but he showed no signs of life.

"Hey," she said, "you gotta get up."

"Hmmm." The boy made banana-chewing sounds with his mouth and rolled over to the other side of the bed.

"Hey!" Claire barked. "*Wake up!*"

She tried to lift him, but he felt more like a sandbag than a ten-year-old boy. Claire placed her bare foot on the guy's back. "*Get*"—she pushed him toward the edge of the bed— "*Off!*" She heard a thud.

"What are ya doin'?" the boy asked.

"Take my blanket and go find a space in the living room with my brother and the rest of his friends," she said.

Once he was gone, Claire shook out her comforter and wrapped it around her. She looked like a sushi roll.

Claire wiggled her hands free and reached for her Elph. She propped her head up against the wooden headboard and snapped a photo of herself. Once the shot was taken, she looked at it on the tiny monitor in the back of the camera and named it "Rock Bottom" because she looked sad and pathetic. Her eyes were hollow and her expression said "mug shot," not "Having a great time in Westchester, wish you were here." This picture was not for her friends in Florida; it was for her. Claire promised she would look at it every time she wanted to believe that she and Massie could be friends.

"So what if Massie is always having fun?" she said to herself. "So what if they're starting a makeup company together? So what if they think I'll never be good enough for them. It's their loss! I'm moving on."

Claire repeated these words over and over again, hoping that by morning she would start to believe them.

```
┌─────────────────────────────────────────────────┐
│                                                   │
│              THE BLOCK ESTATE                      │
│            OUTSIDE THE MAIN HOUSE                  │
│                 11:50 A.M.                         │
│                September 6th                       │
│                                                   │
└─────────────────────────────────────────────────┘
```

Claire sat on a cement block beside a stone statue of a lion. There was an identical one to the left of her, but she chose to sit on the one in the direct sunlight.

She was wearing the dark denim flair jeans the nurse had given her and a white T-shirt with baby blue rhinestones around the neck. It was the closest thing she had to something Massie would wear, which was probably what Layne would be expecting. Luckily the jeans were long enough to cover ninety percent of the Keds.

A black Jaguar pulled into the driveway, but Claire didn't notice Layne. She was too busy trying to get a better look at the really cute guy in the passenger seat. A head of messy hair and a brown leather jacket were all she needed to see to know that he was a WB guy—hot, dangerous, and surprisingly vulnerable.

Layne waved frantically from the backseat while she gathered her stuff. Claire waved back with one hand and checked her bangs with the other.

"Claire, this is my dad, Eric," Layne said when she stepped out of the car.

"Nice to meet you," Claire said to the driver.

"And this is my brother, Chris." Layne pointed to a guy in the front seat.

Chris leaned over his father's seat so he could see Claire.

"What's up?" Chris brushed his floppy, blond hair out of his eyes and gave Claire a brilliant smile.

"Uh, you know." Claire instantly hated herself for sounding so lame.

"Nice pool," Chris said.

"Thanks." Claire looked down at her jeans and let out a modest giggle just in case he thought her response sounded conceited.

"Remember, no swimming," Eric told his daughter. "Not until that ear infection is gone."

"Don't worry." Layne winked.

"Layne Jane Abeley, I mean it. *No Swimming!*" he said.

All of the sudden a flashbulb went off in Claire's head. Layne's last name was Abeley. Her brother was Chris. That meant this was Chris Abeley. *Theee* Chris Abeley.

Claire lowered her head closer to the car window. "You don't go to Briarwood, do you?" she asked.

"Yup, I'm a freshman!" he said with exaggerated enthusiasm.

"My brother just started in the middle school. He's much younger than you, but his name is Todd Lyons, you know, in case you happen to meet him." Claire realized she was rambling and couldn't tell if it was because his eyes were so blue or because she could not believe she was talking to the guy Massie was in love with. He was like a minicelebrity.

"You kidding me? I know Todd. I love that kid. He spitballed a raisin right at the headmaster's eye and then escaped down the hall. Turns out I got blamed because I was standing there when it happened and I couldn't stop laughing," he said. This time his enthusiasm was genuine. "I had to serve detention after school for that, but it was worth it."

"Well, that sounds like Todd, all right. Hey, wanna, come say hi to him?" Claire said. "He's over by the pool."

"Absolutely," Chris said. "Dad, I'll be right back."

When Claire got to the side of the house, she glanced up to make sure Massie was still in her bedroom. As soon as she saw her standing in the window, Claire did everything she could to get her attention.

"Todd! TODD! Look who's here," she called. She didn't care if her brother heard, as long as Massie did.

"Looks like he's feeling better." Layne gave a sincere smile.

It took Claire a second to realize what Layne was talking about. "Oh yeah, he's fine," she said. "Thank God!"

"Heyyyy, buddy," Chris Abeley said when he saw Todd riding an inflatable dolphin in the pool.

Claire saw Massie's curtains move to the side of her window. Showtime.

"Oh my God, Chris." Claire grabbed Chris and looked him straight in the eye. "There's something totally gross in your hair. Let me get it out for you." She lifted her hand toward his face and slowly brushed his long bangs to the side of his forehead. Then she ran her fingers through his shaggy hair. Above her, the curtains swung shut.

"Is it gone?" Chris Abeley asked Claire.

"Yeah, it's gone," Claire said. "I hear gross stuff in your hair is good luck, though."

She never thought she'd be the type of person who would resort to mind games, but then again, she'd never imagined she'd be in a situation where she would need them. Claire felt pleased with herself but also sort of sick.

"Well, I better get going," Chris said. "I'm going riding this afternoon."

After Chris was gone, Layne picked up a dandelion, closed her eyes, and blew the fuzz into the wind. "Wanna make a wish?" Layne asked. She snapped another flower from the ground and handed it to Claire.

"Do I ever." Claire shut her eyes tight and then blew hard enough to bust a lung. "There. Your brother seems really nice."

"Yeah, he's pretty cool," Layne said. "You should see how happy Fawn is now that he's back from boarding school."

"Who's Fawn?" Claire asked. "Your dog?"

"Hardly," Layne said. "She's his disgustingly beautiful girlfriend. They've been dating since the seventh grade."

As soon as Claire heard that, she searched the ground for more dandelions.

"These things are great!" she said, her hands full of rubbery green stems. "They totally work!"

They walked through the ravine in the woods behind the house, taking pictures of creeks, each other, and bugs. They sat on a fallen tree trunk so Layne could eat oatmeal from her thermos while Claire watched in disgust, craving Gummy Feet.

She thought about the what-would-you-rather question Massie had asked at the sleepover—no friends versus friends who hate you—only now she wished there'd been a choice (c), to have one true friend even if everyone else openly hated her. Claire would have picked that.

"Why would I be making it up?" Massie shouted into her Motorola. She was in the middle of a heated four-way call.

"I just can't believe Slow Layne is Chris Abeley's sister," Dylan said.

"I can't believe Claire was stroking his hair!" Alicia sounded mad.

"If we'd left your house a half hour later, we would have seen the whole thing," Kristen said.

Massie was looking in the mirror, wondering what she would look like with bangs. She folded the front of her hair in half and pinned it across her forehead. She stepped back and tried to see herself through Chris's eyes. *Who knows?* Maybe bangs were his thing. But she decided it looked like she was wearing a visor and took it down.

"Hold on. You don't think he likes Claire, do you?" Dylan asked.

"Impossible," Massie said. "Right?"

"Puh-lease, he's giving her the time of day because she's the first person who's ever been nice to his sister," Dylan said.

Massie was about to ask Kristen what she thought of the whole situation, but just then a voice in the background called out, "Kristen, it's been six minutes."

"I know, Mom, I was just hanging up," Kristen called. "Okay, well, thanks for helping me with that homework question. I get it now. Talk to you later, bye." She always did that when her mother caught her talking on the phone any longer than her five-minute allowance.

"What are you going to do?" Alicia asked with a trace of panic in her voice.

"Anything my new best friend Layne wants," Massie said. "I should go. Chris Abeley left my house twenty minutes ago and should be at Galwaugh by now. I don't want to miss him. Wish me luck!" She hung up the phone without saying goodbye. Ten minutes later, one final look in the mirror, and Massie was ready to ride. Her custom-made evergreen riding jacket and her Hermés riding crop gave her that extra confidence she needed. That, and her conversation cheat sheet.

I CAN TALK TO A 15-YEAR-OLD ABOUT . . .	I CANNOT TALK TO A 15-YEAR-OLD ABOUT . . .
PS2, XBOX, GAMECUBE	NINTENDO
HOUSE PARTIES	BIRTHDAY PARTIES
LAYNE—HIS SUPER-COOL SISTER	INSANE LAYNE—HIS SALVATION-ARMY- LOVING, OATMEAL- OBSESSED SISTER

The Galwaugh Farms main office was very Ralph Lauren. It was pure rustic log cabin on the outside and *très*

Aspen ranch on the inside. Colorful Indian blankets were haphazardly placed over deep leather chairs, and old hardcover books lined the wood shelves. Even in the dead of summer the smell of pine was overwhelming. To Massie it was a home away from home. She checked in and very casually asked the girl at the desk what trail Tricky (and Chris Abeley) was on. When she found out it was Shady Lane, she ran to the stables and got Brownie.

"Ready for our first double date?" Massie asked Brownie. "Do you have any idea how cute you and Tricky look together? So, what do you think of me and Chris?" She looked over her shoulder after she said that to make sure he wasn't sneaking up on her again. "You don't think he likes Claire, do you?" she whispered. "She's probably way too plain for him, right?"

Unlike Bean, Brownie wasn't much of a conversationalist. But his ears were always wide open.

Shady Lane was lined on either side with giant weeping willows and was always dark and chilly. Massie had wanted to wear her long blazer and riding gloves because she knew how the pine trees blocked the sun this time of year, but she didn't want Chris Abeley to think she'd put too much thought into her outfit. She wanted everything about her to seem effortless.

"Woo-hooooo!" a voice hollered from behind her.

Sure enough, Chris Abeley and Tricky were rushing toward them.

"How did you get behind me?" Massie shouted over her

shoulder. She tapped Brownie with her riding crop while she spoke, hoping to pick up speed.

"I was hiding in the bushes," Chris Abeley said.

"Did you hear what I was saying to Brownie?" Massie asked. She prayed the answer was no.

"Wait, I thought you didn't talk to your horse." Chris smiled. "You are so busted!"

Massie had no choice but to laugh.

"Last one to the lake talks to horses!" Chris said. "No shortcuts." And away he went.

Massie loved the way Chris rode. One hand held the blue New York Yankees baseball hat on his head and the other gripped the reins.

"This is it, Brownie, get 'em!" Massie said. The horse let out a whinny and turned around and started charging toward Tricky.

Massie pulled up beside Chris Abeley and stuck her arm out as far as it would go. Her charm bracelet nearly fell off, but she wiggled it back toward her elbow to keep it from sliding off. She lined herself up next to Chris Abeley and shouted, "Heads up!" before snatching the NY Yankees hat right off his head. In what appeared to be one smooth motion she undid her helmet, strapped it to her saddle, and slapped the cap over her blowing hair.

She'd learned this trick in her second year of riding camp, but he didn't have to know that. Massie could tell by the gleam in his eyes that she'd passed that test. It was time to move on.

"What about you? What do you like doing in your free time?"

"I hang out with my friends, listen to music, and you know, I like entertaining when my parents are out of town." he gave a mischievous grin.

"What do you mean by *entertaining?*" Massie asked. She was afraid of the answer because it would mean she, as his future girlfriend, would be expected to do whatever it was that he did while he was entertaining, and she wasn't sure if she was ready for that (or even knew what "that" was).

"You know, party stuff," he said.

"Sure," Massie said.

They got deeper into the thickening woods and Tricky started grunting through her nose. She was shaking her head yes and no as if there was a pesky fly circling her, but there wasn't. Tricky jerked forward, wanting to run, but Chris tightened the reins and held her back so they could keep trotting alongside Brownie and Massie. This was a good sign. Massie took it to mean he was having fun and wasn't ready to leave. It was the perfect time to hit him up with the golden question.

"You said your last name was Abeley, right?" she asked. She squinted when she asked the question, hoping it made her look sincerely puzzled.

"Yeah," he said.

"Are you by chance related to Layne Abeley?" Massie asked.

"She's my little sister."

"That's what I thought," she said, slapping her thigh. "I love Layne. She was actually at my house this morning."

"That's *your* house?" Chris Abeley said. "I was there too. My dad dropped her off and then gave me a ride here." He paused for a second. "Wait, I thought her friend Claire lived there."

"That's sooo funny." Massie laughed. "N-n-n-no, she lives in my guest house. Let's just say we're helping her family get through some tough times." She rubbed her thumb against her index and middle fingers, indicating it was a money thing.

"Ohhh." He sounded like he felt sorry for her. "Well, you're lucky—she seems really cool and her brother is a wild man. He reminds me of myself when I was that age."

"Really?" Massie pulled an elastic out of her side pocket and after a few twists of the wrist her hair was tied in a loose bun that bobbed up and down on the back of her head.

"I love when girls do that," Chris said.

"What?" Massie asked.

"That crazy thing with their hair," he said, wiggling his long fingers in the air. When his hand fell to his side, he just looked at her peacefully, allowing his smile to slowly fade. Massie could see that he was truly in awe.

His puppy dog expression worried her just a little bit, like maybe he was falling too quickly. She didn't have a list to tell her how to act during awkward moments, so she did the next-best thing and changed the subject.

"Whatever happened to our race?" she asked. "On your mark, get set—"

"GO!" Chris Abeley shouted before shooting ahead.

"CHEATER!" Massie shouted after him.

"LOSER!" Chris shouted back.

Loser was one thing Massie would not allow herself to be called, even as a joke. She leaned forward to become aerodynamic and gave Brownie the command to run as fast as he possibly could. His thundering hooves pounded the trail, snapping twigs and kicking up dirt each time they beat the ground.

"Looks like you're a cheater *and* a loser," Massie said. She was out of breath.

"You're pretty good for a filly," he said, pretending to crack his knuckles. "My sister got on a horse once and started bawling her eyes out the second it started moving."

"Was she scared?" Massie asked, trying to sound concerned.

"*No,* she just felt bad for the horse," Chris Abeley said, rolling his eyes.

Massie giggled but stopped as soon as she noticed him staring at her hand.

"What?" she asked.

Chris Abeley didn't answer.

He leaned over and reached for her tiny wrist with his big guy hand. A tingle shot through her entire body when he touched her and she imagined getting electrocuted felt the same. Everything around her became silent.

"Charming." He lifted each charm with the tip of his index finger.

Massie could feel him looking straight at her even

though her eyes were fixated on the silver microphone the Lyonses gave her. She pulled her arm away before he could notice it.

"You should bring her out one time," Massie said.

She skillfully managed to look at Chris while her fingers raced to unhook the hideous charm. When she got it off, she casually released it, like a gum wrapper she was ashamed to throw on the ground.

"Who?" Chris Abeley asked.

He inched his body back into the middle of the saddle without taking his eyes off her. She felt paralyzed, like he was sucking her soul.

"Layne," Massie said. "Bring her out next weekend and I'll give her a riding lesson."

"I gotta see *that*," Chris said.

"You're on," Massie said.

"Good," Chris said. "It's a date."

Massie waved goodbye and rode off as fast as she possibly could. She wanted to get away before he noticed she still had his hat.

Layne plopped down in the cushy automatic massage chair.

"Four speeds," the pedicurist offered. She handed the remote control to Layne, but she couldn't take it. Her hands were too full.

"Layne, you have to pick *one* color." Massie felt like she was speaking to a child.

"I think it would be cool if every toe was different," Layne said. "Don't you?"

"No," Massie said.

"Yeah, I guess it's kind of stupid," Layne said. She put the bottles back on the modern looking chrome shelf. "Which one do *you* like?" she asked Massie.

"Baby's Breath," Massie said. "It's a good color for beginners—pink but not too pink, sheer but not too sheer."

The girls soaked their feet in warm soapy water and flipped through magazines. All around them fashionably dressed women were getting their nails done by the best manicurists in all of Westchester.

"This tickles," Layne said. She yanked her feet away every time the pedicurist tried to exfoliate them with a pumice stone.

Massie looked at the poor woman, who was trying

desperately to scrub Layne's foot, and rolled her eyes.

Massie was glad she had the sense to call ahead and make sure no other OCD girls had four o'clock appointments. She wanted this tryst with Layne kept below the radar.

"Thanks again for bringing me here. This place is beautiful, like a shiny forest!" Layne said, referring to sparkling chrome fixtures and the lush looking potted plants. "And thanks for pulling me aside after gym to let me know I have snaggle toes."

"No problem," Massie said. "That's what friends are for." Massie could see Layne's face light up as soon as she heard the word *friends*. This was really just too easy.

"Your toes are looking so much better already."

"Iiiiii knnnoooowwww," Layne said. Her seat was now vibrating at high speed.

"Oh, by the way," Massie said without looking up from the pages of *People*. "Did your brother tell you we met last weekend?"

"Nnnnnnnnnnnooooooooooo," Layne said.

Massie slapped the magazine closed and held it against her thigh. "We went riding together," she said. "Are you sure he didn't mention it?"

"Yyyyeeeaaahhh," Layne said.

"You must not be very close." Massie gave a sympathetic smile.

Layne shut off the chair and stared directly into Massie's eyes.

"He's my best friend," Layne said. "We tell each other everything."

Massie knew she must have hit a nerve and decided not to push any further. It was important that she keep on Layne's good side.

"I know, he told me," Massie said. "He even said he wished you liked riding so you could spend more time together."

"He did?" Layne said.

"Oh yeah." Massie nodded and made her voice sound very intense, like she had been moved by the depths of Chris Abeley's love for his sister. "Hey, I have an idea. Why don't you let me teach you how to ride next weekend? Then we can all spend the day together."

"Come on." Layne slapped her hand against her heart. "You would do all that for *me?*"

"Of course." Massie raised her hand to her head and smoothed down her already perfect hair. "Who *else* would I be doing it for?"

Claire stared at the microwave. The clock showed double numbers, which meant she had one minute to make as many wishes as she could before it became 11:12 A.M. She asked for friends at OCD, good grades, Massie's approval, which would lead to Kristen, Alicia, and Dylan's approval, which would lead to everyone else's approval, the lead in the school play (whatever it was), new clothes, a different carpool, braworthy boobs by Christmas, neater handwriting, and faster-growing hair.

"Shouldn't Layne be here by now?" Judi asked. She stood by the stove dipping strawberries into a pot of bubbling chocolate one by one and then laying them out on a sheet of wax paper. It was her turn to make dessert for the book club she'd joined.

"She's not coming," Claire said. She sat at the kitchen table mindlessly rolling and unrolling a cherry print place mat.

"What was her excuse this time?" Judi asked sympathetically. "Is something wrong between you and Layne?"

"No, she's just busy with 'her new' best friend, Massie," Claire said. She was so upset, she put air quotes around "her new" instead of "best friend."

Judi glanced at the place mat Claire was mangling, with a look of concern in her eye.

"I don't understand. Can't you all hang out together?" Judi asked.

"Gee, that's a great idea," Claire said. "Come to think of it, the president could really use your help with that crisis in the Middle East."

Claire heard a snicker come from under the table. She leaned over and found Todd curled up in a ball with his hand over his mouth.

"All kidding aside, do you want me to talk to Massie's mom about this?" Judi said. "I mean, I see no reason why they can't include you. Maybe it's an oversight."

Todd laughed through his nose.

"I will give you everything I have in my savings account if you promise not to talk to *anyone* about this," Claire said. "I'm fine. I swear."

Claire pushed her seat back from the table and stepped lightly on her brother's hand as she stood up. She watched him squirm through the cracks on the wood table and choked back her laughter.

"I think Todd is by the pool," Judi offered. "Why don't you join him for a swim?"

"Maybe," Claire said. "He pees in the pool, you know."

Claire heard his gasp and pressed her foot down one last time.

"I'm going to change."

Claire thought about how badly she wanted to tell her

mother the truth, what a relief it would be to finally be honest, admit that she *had* no friends. She'd *thought* she had Layne but then *Massie* had swooped in stolen her. Ever since Massie had started inviting her places, Layne had all but disappeared. Claire was too embarrassed to admit this to her mother, so she kept her mouth shut.

Instead she wiped the tears from her eyes and slipped into her favorite bikini—the denim-looking bottoms with the belt and a white triangle top. She'd gotten it on sale at Target, for fifteen dollars, and it usually made her feel like a million bucks. But today, a beautiful Saturday afternoon when she had no one to hang out with but her little brother, she felt like fifteen cents.

Chris Abeley and Massie trotted along Shady Lane, constantly looking over their shoulders to make sure Layne was still behind them. She had refused to get on her horse, insisting that the mare much preferred a leisurely walk.

"Layne, are you sure you don't want to at least *try* riding Trixie?" Massie asked. "I'm sure she won't mind."

"No, I'm having fun taking pictures of flowers and stuff," Layne answered.

"That's cool. It's just that I have to be home at one o'clock for a meeting and at this rate we won't be out of here for another three hours." Massie grit her teeth and tried to force a smile. It came out looking more like a grimace.

"I didn't know you had to leave early," Chris Abeley said. "I packed some sandwiches, hoping we could all have a picnic at the falls."

"If we ever get there," Massie mumbled under her breath.

"I heard that!" Layne said.

"I was only kidding, Layne," Massie said. "I would love to have a picnic. I can be a *little* late, I guess."

"Good," Chris Abeley said. "By the way, are you ever going to bring back my Yankees hat? Layne told me you wear it every day to school."

His face was beaming and Massie couldn't tell if he was serious about wanting it back or if he was just flirting.

"I do not." Massie felt her face getting hot. "Layne, why did you tell him that?"

"Because it's true," Layne said. "I thought he'd be flattered."

"The hat I wear isn't your brother's, it's mine," Massie said. "Chris, I will gladly return your hat. I'll bring it next weekend. It's too big for me anyway."

"Oh, I forgot to tell you I can't ride next weekend," Chris said. "I have a lacrosse game."

"I can ride," Layne said.

But Massie pretended she didn't hear that.

"Hey," Layne shouted. She was crouched down at the edge of the trail. "Look what I found."

Chris and Massie stopped their horses and waited patiently for Layne and Trixie to catch up to them. The way Layne walked the tiny object over to Chris made her look like a lawyer approaching the bench.

"It looks like a little microphone," Layne said.

"Massie, isn't this yours?" Chris Abeley said. He handed the charm to Massie, making an extra effort not to drop it. "I saw it on your bracelet before. You must have lost it while we were riding last time."

"Do you want me to put it on for you?" Layne asked.

"Thanks, Layne." Massie knew her tone sounded irritated and made every effort not sound ungrateful.

"Charmed," Layne said with a British accent. "Get it?"

Chris cracked up and Massie mustered up the best fake laugh she could under the circumstances.

"That's some luck that Layne found it, huh?" Chris said once he stopped laughing.

"Yeah, totally," Massie answered. *Some* bad *luck*, she thought. She had ditched that tacky thing a week ago, yet somehow it was back to haunt her. Not unlike the tacky family that gave it to her.

It wasn't even noon yet, but it was hot, hot, hot. Claire walked over to the Blocks' pool, figuring she'd take a quick dip since nobody was around, but when she got there she saw a long buffet table, draped in a white tablecloth, set up in front of the cabanas. She stopped in her tracks. Covering the table were platters of mini-sandwiches, pasta salad, and chilled soups wrapped in saran wrap to keep the flies away. It looked like the Blocks were in the middle of setting up for a party.

A few inches away from the food, closer to the silver-ware, Inez had fanned four notebooks out like magazines. Each one said GLAMBITION in big bold type. Suddenly Claire didn't feel like swimming.

"What's going on?" Claire asked Inez.

Beads of sweat had formed on the woman's upper lip and she was squinting from the sun.

"Massie is having a meeting," Inez answered.

Just as Inez said that, Claire heard the pool gate click open. Alicia, Kristen, and Dylan walked in wearing bathing suits, sarongs and flip-flops. They moved slowly and scraped the wooden soles of their shoes across the pave-ment as they made their way over to the deck chairs.

Dylan dragged two chairs across the deck and pushed

them together, and all three of them piled on. Their tangled arms and legs made them look like one big spider.

"Hey, Claire, who made your bikini?" Alicia asked.

It was practically the first time she had heard them refer to her by name. But she had to be careful: It could easily be a trap. Claire had learned enough in the last few weeks to know that admitting it was from Target would have terrible repercussions.

"Please tell me you're kidding," Claire said.

Alicia looked to Kristen and Dylan with a hint of panic on her face, but they immediately looked away.

"It's an Astrud," Claire said, and paused as if she were waiting for a sign of recognition from Alicia. "You know, from Brazil?"

"Duh!" Alicia smacked herself in the forehead. "I knew it looked familiar. I just saw a whole story on her in *Teen Vogue*."

"You mean *him!*" Claire hoped she wasn't going too far with her lie.

"Seriously, Leesh," Kristen said.

"Everyone knows Astrud is a guy," Dylan added.

"I must have just spaced," Alicia said. "I've had a bad headache all day and I can't think properly."

Kristen started twirling her hair. Dylan reached for a bag of sunflower seeds. And Alicia began massaging her temples. Claire knew they were each secretly wondering how they could have possibly missed the news about Astrud. And Astrud didn't even exist!

"Where do you think she is *this* time?" Kristen asked.

"What?" Claire asked. But the girls were back in their tangle and she realized they weren't talking to her anymore.

"Whatever it is, I'm sure it has everything to do with Chris," Alicia said. "I'm sorry, I mean Chris *Abeley*." She took her sunglasses off as she spoke and put them right back on when she finished. "I'm so tired of having to say both of his names."

"Well, if she blows off one more Glambition meeting, I'm going to fire her," Kristen said. "This project is worth seventy-five percent of my grade and if I fail, I'm dead."

"Why do you think she never invites us to hang out with them?" Dylan asked.

"Because she wants quuuuaaaaaa-lity time with Chrisabeley," Kristen said. She blended his two names together so they sounded like one. The other girls laughed.

But Claire knew what was really going on. Massie didn't want them to find out she was spending time with Layne. She'd seen Massie avoid Layne at school by using the same techniques she had used to shake Claire—sudden detours to the bathroom, engaging in must-have conversations with B-listers when Layne approached, or acting like she was in the middle of a crucial cell phone call and just couldn't be interrupted.

"Do you think she's going to start hanging out with high school girls?" Dylan asked. "You know, now that she's so in with Chrisabeley."

"Not if she keeps wearing that cheesy Yankees hat," Kristen said. "I remember a time when the only initials she wore were YSL, LV, and CC. I'm not sure I can handle NYY."

"Please, I saw you checking the price on a Yankees hat at the mall last Wednesday," Alicia said. "I even saw you try it on when you thought I was checking my hair in the mirror."

Claire felt a jumble of nerves rolling in her stomach, but she opened her mouth and forced herself to say the coolest thing she could think to say. "I hate to interrupt, but it wouldn't kill you to have a little fun while you're waiting," Claire shouted.

They looked up from their cluster in shock, but no one said a word. The only sounds were sunflower seeds cracking between Dylan's teeth.

Claire managed to stroll past them with grace and nonchalance, but on the inside she was still reeling from her gutsy outburst.

She stepped up on the diving board with the poise of an Olympic diver and padded to the very edge. She bounced a few times to test the spring of the board and waited for the wind to shift.

They were watching.

She moved to the back of the board and placed her arms stiffly by her sides. One quick hop and she was airborne. Her body curled into a tight ball and after one flip, she snapped open like a jackknife and landed a perfect dive.

Claire surfaced to applause.

One by one the girls untied their sarongs, kicked off their flip-flops, and pulled their bathing suits out of their butts before jumping in. Alicia ran into the cabana and blasted the radio. Britney Spears's "Oops! . . . I Did It Again" was playing and even though the girls couldn't stand her anymore, they all seemed glad it was on.

They stood by the edge of the pool and sang along to the chorus.

Oops! . . . I did it again

I played with your heart, got lost in the game

Oh baby, baby . . .

"Oops!" Dylan shouted as she pushed Alicia into the pool. She was still wearing her shirt, but Claire had a feeling she would have stayed covered up even if she hadn't been taken by surprise.

"Claire, you're not the only one who can dive," Dylan said. "Check this out."

Dylan ran to the diving board and spastically stumbled to the edge. She fell in the water like a brick.

"That's what I like to call the drunk diver," she said when she came up for air.

Everyone laughed freely, especially Claire.

Alicia twirled off the board with her arms over her head, doing what she called the ballerina dive.

Kristen pretended to be Britney. She shook her hips from side to side and let her arm swing in front of her while she walked toward the water, singing.

Oops! . . . You think I'm in love

That I'm sent from above

I'm not that innocent!

She landed with a splash right as the song ended.

"Whoo-hoo!" the girls shouted.

But Claire's next move stole the show. She pulled down her bathing suit, flashed her butt, and screamed, "Bottoms up!"

Another Britney song came on the radio and the girls bleated with excitement.

"STRONGER!" they shouted.

There's nothing you can do or say, baby
I've had enough
I'm not your property as from today—

They acted out the lyrics and sang to each other like seasoned video stars. Claire was so happy, her teeth were chattering.

Arms were raised high in the air and butts were shaking when they noticed Massie standing by the edge of the pool. Bean was at her side.

The laughter faded fast.

"Britney?" Massie said. Her nose was scrunched up like she had caught a whiff of something foul.

Alicia jumped out of the pool and turned off the music.

"Where were you? You're an hour late." Kristen had successfully masked her disappointment with concern.

"I know, I'm so sorry. We rode a new trail and got lost and couldn't get decent cell service. I was terrified. If Chris wasn't a trained Boy Scout, we would have *died* out there," she said. She lifted Bean off the ground and held her close.

The girls chose to believe her because it was a lot safer than calling her bluff. One by one they stepped out of the pool, hugged her, and told her how happy they were that she was alive.

"We should probably get started because my dad is coming to get me in an hour," Kristen said.

They walked over to the buffet table, removed the plastic wrap from the trays, and began filling their plates with food. Everything Massie took she also added to Bean's bowl. Claire was not invited to join them, so she got out of the pool and acted invisible while she dried off in the sun.

"What were you laughing about with leechy Lyons?" Massie asked. She reached for the pitcher of lemonade.

"We were laughing because she had a huge booger hanging out of her nose while she was swimming," Alicia lied. She looked at the others to make sure they wouldn't blow her cover.

Claire, who was standing alone by the diving board, pinched her nose just in case it was true.

Massie leaned into Kristen and whispered something in her ear. When Massie finished talking, Kristen grabbed the crystal saltshaker off the table and walked over to Claire, who was lying facedown on her towel. She stood above Claire and started dumping salt on her.

"What are you doing?" Claire asked, sitting up in shock.

"Salt gets rid of leeches," Kristen answered.

Massie watched with a satisfied grin on her face.

Alicia slapped a piece of lox on Claire's back and explained, "So does smoked salmon."

"Nothing works better than gazpacho," Dylan said while pouring the cold vegetable soup on Claire's head.

"Dylan, be careful," Massie said with mock concern, "those Target bathing suits are really hard to clean."

Claire felt her eyes tingling, which always happened when she was about to cry. She bit her lip; she would *not* give these girls the satisfaction. Instead, she forced herself to walk calmly over to the outdoor shower, even though she was so upset she could barely breathe. She held her head high and didn't even bothering to wipe the green pepper chunk off her cheek.

Over at the table the other girls were strangely quiet. And then all of the sudden, Kristen broke the silence.

"I think we should launch our first Glambitious product in a week," Kristen said loudly. "The day our grade goes to the city for the *All My Children* taping."

"Kristen, that's perfect," Massie agreed. "We can sell on the bus. We'll make a fortune!" She swallowed hard and tried to sound cheerful.

"What's our first product going to be?" Dylan asked.

"I think we should make a sugar-and-orange body scrub," Alicia said.

"No, it should be something that everyone can use on the bus, like cheek tint or lip gloss," Kristen said.

"Homemade lip gloss!" Massie said. "*J'adore!*"

Kristen punched numbers on her calculator. "Let's see, we can probably get most of the ingredients from our own kitchens, so I'm only going to budget ten dollars for that, thirty dollars for plastic pill containers that we'll use to hold the gloss, ten dollars for labels, and sixty dollars for labor, which is you guys." She entered a few more numbers and was ready to announce the retail price.

"So, if we sell thirty lip glosses at five-fifty a jar, Glambitious, Inc., will make fifty-five dollars profit on its first day," Kristen said, her eyes gleaming at the possibility. "Let's start making everything next Friday. That will give us plenty of time to try different recipes before the field trip."

"Done."

"Done."

"And done."

Claire sat in her bedroom with the lights off. The sun had started to set earlier and earlier every day, which added to her feelings of loneliness. She could see Massie in her bedroom talking on the phone and brushing Bean, but the limited view she had from her window offered little insight. From where Claire sat, Massie looked just like a regular, albeit very beautiful, seventh-grade girl, not the monster Claire now knew she was.

Claire e-mailed pictures of OCD, the changing leaves, and her flowery old lady wallpaper to Sarah and Sari with a note that said, *Save me.* Then she lay there, quietly thinking about Massie and how much mean stuff she'd done, thinking about how much Massie *deserved* some sort of payback.

At 8:13 P.M. Claire saw Massie turn out her bedroom light. She was leaving for her nightly walk with her father and Bean. The walk lasted about fifteen minutes because they were always back at 8:30 P.M. This gave Claire exactly seventeen minutes.

Claire crawled out her bedroom window and down the white trellis on the side of the house. She crept across the lawn and thought about how hard she'd tried to be friends with Massie. Then she thought about what had happened at the pool. Then she thought about how Massie had stolen Layne.

Claire let herself in through the side door.

"Hi, Kendra. Can I run up to Massie's room and borrow her science book? She said it would be okay." Claire smiled calmly, but inside, she was a bundle of nervous energy.

"Sure," Kendra said.

Claire could barely believe she was doing this, sneaking into Massie's room. She, of course, had no idea what she was going to do when she got there, but just the fact that she was entering without Massie's permission was pretty exciting.

The bedroom had more purple in it since Claire had seen it last. Purple pillows, a purple rug, and a purple iMac were all new additions to the otherwise white room.

Claire heard the sound of a door creak open and she froze. She was so scared of getting caught that she couldn't even think of a place to hide. She heard the sound again and finally realized that it was coming from Massie's computer. Someone from her IM buddy list was online. She looked up the profile of the person named HolaGurrl.

It was Alicia.

HOLAGURRL: ? R U UP 2

Claire jumped away from the computer like it was alive. She couldn't believe such a perfect opportunity had presented itself so quickly. She twisted her bracelets and paced the room, trying to burn off some of the adrenaline that was rushing through her body. She pressed her ear against Massie's bedroom door to make sure no one was right outside and then hurried over to the computer. She had always wanted to know what it felt like to be Massie Block. She breathed in and out. In and out. Then she typed.

MASSIEKUR: USUAL. U?

Claire hit ENTER and jumped back as if the keys were burning hot.

HOLAGURRL: BOUT TO SHOP ONLINE.
WANNA DO IT 2GETHER? I'LL CALL U.

Claire pushed back her bracelets and started typing.

MASSIEKUR: NO.
I'M GOING TO HANG @ CLAIRE'S.
MAYBE WATCH MOVIES.
LUV HER NOW! SO FUN!
G2G.
BTW—LET'S WEAR SHORTS OVER
TIGHTS MONDAY.
JUST SAW IT IN 17. SUPER CUTE!
TELL K&D.
HOLAGURRL: SERIOUS?
MASSIEKUR: BOUT ???
HOLAGURRL: ALL OF IT!
MASSIEKUR: TOTALLY.LAYTAH ☺

Claire made sure the wireless mouse was exactly where Massie had left it and then started to plan her escape. She opened the door slowly and stuck her head out far enough to have a quick look around. She thought she could hear someone breathing but told herself she was imagining it. She stuck her toe out in the hallway like she was testing water to make sure it wasn't too cold before jumping in. As soon as her leg hit the floor, something grabbed her ankle and she let out a loud scream.

"Claire, is everything okay?" Kendra yelled from downstairs.

"Yeah, I'm fine," Claire shouted back. But she wasn't.

Todd was standing right in front of her with a big cocky grin across his face.

"I can't believe you followed me," Claire whispered.

"Shhh," Todd said. "You'll get caught."

Claire's first instinct was to punch him. She raised her fist but withdrew at the thought of Massie coming home and finding them beating each other outside her bedroom door.

"We better get out of here," Claire said. "I'll kick your butt later."

"Correction," Todd said. "You'll *kiss* my butt later. Unless of course you want this little secret of yours getting out."

Claire's mouth shot open in protest.

"That'll teach you not to spy on people," Todd said. He slapped Claire lightly on the arm and led them both to safety.

Massie stood with her arms crossed. She was wearing a black silk dress with a mandarin collar over faded Miss Sixtys. She had a half smile on her face while she watched Claire hoist herself into the backseat of the Range Rover. Claire was wearing forest green tights, dark denim jean shorts, and a white T-shirt.

"I didn't know the drama department was holding auditions for *Peter Pan* today," Massie said.

"Well, you obviously knew about the auditions for *Miss Saigon*," Claire fired back.

Massie was impressed by Claire's comeback, but she couldn't help wondering why she was suddenly so full of confidence. Her outfit was an outrage, yet she acted like she had just made number one on *People*'s best-dressed list.

Massie could hear her friends laughing already and couldn't wait for them to see Claire's latest creation.

They waited their usual five minutes for Alicia to walk through the gates and, as always, they sat in silence.

"Ehmagod!" Massie said.

Isaac and Claire turned to see what she was looking at.

Alicia sauntered toward the car, her hair blowing off her face like a model, in a shampoo commercial. She was wearing

145

tomato red tights, cutoff Levi's, a black vest, and black strappy shoes. Her outfit was ridiculous, but in true Alicia fashion, she still looked beautiful.

"What are you wearing?" Alicia asked Massie.

"You're asking *me?*" Massie sounded surprised.

"Why do you look all *ELLEgirl* instead of *Seventeen?*" Alicia asked.

Massie knew there had to be a logical answer for this but decided she would come to it on her own. It was better than asking and sounding clueless.

"Bean scratched my tights as I was leaving and I had to change at the last minute," Massie lied.

Massie wondered how Claire, of all people, had managed to wear the same horrible outfit as Alicia. Or maybe the better question was, how had Alicia managed to wear the same horrible outfit as Claire?

Massie turned toward the backseat, hoping a stare-down with Claire would give way to some answers. Their eyes met, but Claire maintained her innocence by flashing a warm smile. A warm smile after what they'd done to her at the pool? Massie should have been suspicious, but her mind was on other things.

Massie spent the ride to Dylan's reviewing her English homework just so she wouldn't have to look at Alicia. But things only got worse.

Dylan wore black tights and black satin shorts and Kristen wore yellow tights and Sevens, which she'd obviously cut the night before, because they were totally uneven.

Massie looked at the row of colorful legs that spread from one end of the car to the other.

"I feel like I'm sitting in a box of Crayolas," she said.

"It sucks that Bean ripped your tights," Kristen said. "Maybe Isaac can pull over somewhere and we can get you another pair. You know, so you won't feel stupid."

"Trust me, I'm not the one who's going to feel stupid." Massie rolled her eyes.

"What's that supposed to mean?" Dylan said.

"Nothing," Massie said. She silently reminded herself to stay cool.

"Claire, I have something for you." Alicia fished around the inside of her Louis Vuitton Cherry Blossom bag and pulled out a cell phone. "It's my dad's old cell phone. It works perfectly."

"Really?" Claire leaned forward, probably to see if Alicia was serious before she accepted it. "Thanks." Claire tried to keep herself from laughing out loud. *This was working. This was actually working.*

"Yeah, no problem, the number is on the inside," Alicia said.

"What about the bill?" Claire asked.

"Puh-lease! My dad's company pays. They won't even notice," Alicia said.

"Claire, here's an invitation to my birthday party next week," Dylan offered. "It's in Manhattan, at the Four Seasons Hotel. There will be a few celebrities there and tons of paparazzi, so we're going shopping this weekend if you want to come."

"Sure!" Claire was bubbling with excitement. She

couldn't believe her little Massie impersonation had worked so well!

Massie, on the other hand, felt faint. *What* the heck was going *on?* She let her friends talk about Dylan's birthday party for the rest of the ride and reviewed her English homework. At the moment it was the only thing that made any sense.

The car pulled up in front of OCD and Massie did a quick scan of the people sitting on the front lawn. Everything appeared to be normal. Not a pair of tights 'n' shorts in sight, not even on the indie girls.

Massie concluded that this was an inside job.

The Crayolas stepped out of the car and walked toward the front doors of OCD. They stood tall and turned up their noses at the "regular" people who hadn't been alerted to the latest trend.

For the first time ever *Massie* looked like one of the outcasts. She wondered if people would think Alicia, Dylan, and Kristen suddenly liked Claire more than her because of how they were dressed. *She* would have.

"Claire, I'll save you a seat in math," Kristen said. "Unless you get there first, then you save me a seat."

" 'Kay." Claire made her way toward her locker. *Victory!*

They all ran off in separate directions, leaving Massie standing by herself in the middle of the hall.

"Massie," a voice yelled from across the corridor. "I'm so glad I found you." It was Layne. "Even though Chris can't ride with you this Saturday, I can. I know last weekend I was lame because I didn't want to ride Trixie, but this time I swear I'll try. And I'll bring my good camera so we can take pictures of—"

"Layne, why don't you take a picture of *this*," Massie said as she flipped Layne the bird. She pulled her into a nearby bathroom and lowered her voice. "I thought I told you not to talk to me at school and that our plans had to stay secret."

"You did, but I thought it was a *joke*," Layne said. "I thought you were *kidding*." Her voice was shaking.

"Yeah? Well, I wasn't," Massie said. "By the way, I can't ride this weekend either, so our plans are off. In fact, they're off for good."

She knew she was being overly mean and she felt bad, but she couldn't stop herself. Her entire world was falling apart.

"Fine. Consider me gone, *forever!*" Layne said. And then she took off down the hall in tears.

Ever since that day, bright-colored tights began popping up on legs around school. Not everyone wore them with jean shorts, but a lot of people did. The skinny girls paired them with miniskirts while others hid them under ripped jeans so the colors would show through. Claire could not believe *she* was responsible for this trend. . . . If they only knew.

Claire sat on her bed and stared out the window that faced Massie's room. She was almost sick with excitement.

8:15 P.M. could not come fast enough.

All day Claire had thought about what IMs she would write to Kristen, Alicia, and Dylan while Massie was out on her nightly walk with Bean. What would she make them wear next? Whom would she tell them to befriend? What gossip would they tell her? She knew she was taking an insane risk sneaking into Massie's room, impersonating her in IMs and telling her friends how to behave. And she knew that what she was doing wasn't exactly "nice" or "fair," but at the same time it felt sinfully good. Besides, they'd treated her terribly, right? So didn't they *deserve* to have a little taste of their own bitchy medicine? Maybe it was a good thing she was doing. Maybe some humbling would make them all nicer people! Claire's rationalizations were interrupted by an electronic rendition of the "Battle Hymn of the Republic." It took Claire a second to realize it was her new cell phone ringing. She pulled it out of her backpack.

"Hey, Alicia." Claire watched herself in the mirror while she spoke. "What are you doing?"

"Trying on some old silver bracelets my mom is getting rid of," Alicia said.

"How old are they?" Claire asked.

"Last season," Alicia said.

Claire looked at the frayed ropes that lay limp on her wrist. The original colors were faded and they were starting to yellow because she wore them in the shower. Why had she never noticed that before? They had to go.

She clipped them off with a nail clipper while Alicia tried to figure out what to keep and what to let her mother pass on to the "help."

Claire saw the light shut off in Massie's bedroom and knew it was time to make her move.

"Alicia, can I call you back in fifteen minutes? I just have to help my mom with something," Claire said.

"Sure, but before I forget," she said, "I called to see if you wanted to go shopping for something to wear to Dylan's party. I feel like spending."

"Of course," Claire said. "I'd never turn down an excuse to spend."

Claire decided she would figure out where she would get money later. For now, she was just happy that she was invited.

She snapped Mr. Rivera's cell phone shut and turned off her lights. It was 8:17 P.M. and Massie would be back in less than fifteen minutes.

She had one leg out the window when she heard a knock on her door.

"What?" Claire said.

"You don't think you're going without me, do you?" Todd said. He let himself into her room and stood in front of her with his fists on his hips like a superhero. He was dressed in black from head to toe.

"No way," Claire said. She swung her leg back inside.

"If I don't go, you don't go," Todd said.

Claire looked at her watch.

"Fine," she said. "But *stay quiet.*"

Claire decided it would probably be better if they snuck by Kendra this time so she wouldn't start to wonder why she was always stopping over when Massie was gone.

They made it up the stairs and into Massie's room without a problem. Todd guarded the door while Claire went straight to the computer. She lowered the volume and composed her first IM. This one was to BigRedHead. It had to be Dylan.

MASSIEKUR: WHAT'S UP?
BIGREDHEAD: BIOLOGY HOMEWORK ☹
MASSIEKUR: WHAT R U WEARING TO YOUR
　　　　　　　 PARTY?
BIGREDHEAD: MAYBE A SUEDE MINI FROM
　　　　　　　　 BARNEY'S CATALOG, PG 23

MASSIEKUR: THINK YOUR LEGS WILL LOOK GOOD
IN A MINI??

Claire couldn't believe she had stooped so low. In a billion years she never thought she'd be the kind of person who would go out of their way to make someone feel bad about their weight. But then again, she'd never imagined she'd be in any of the situations she'd been in as of late.

BIGREDHEAD: WHY?
MASSIEKUR: JUST ASKING.
G2G, CLAIRE JUST STOPPED BY
BIGREDHEAD: WAIT, DO YOU THINK I HAVE FAT
LEGS??????????????????????????
BIGREDHEAD: MASSIE!
BIGREDHEAD: R U THERE?
BIGREDHEAD HAS SIGNED OFF 8:29 P.M.

Claire shut Dylan's message to make sure Massie wouldn't find it and left with Todd as quickly as they came.

The next morning in the car Dylan was silent. She wore a long skirt that dragged along the ground and a bulky sweatshirt.

"Laundry day?" Alicia asked when she saw Dylan.

"*No.*" Dylan glared at Massie. "I'm just cold."

Just like the night before, Claire crept into Massie's room. Kristen was next, but she was going to be a little tougher than Dylan because Claire had no idea what her soft spot was. She knew Kristen cared a lot about her grades, but that was really it.

Claire was not surprised to see SexySportsBabe logged on. Every night she had visited Massie's computer, Kristen was online, probably doing homework.

"The coast is clear," Todd said.

"Thanks. Give me the signal at 8:27 P.M.," Claire said.

Todd gave a quick nod, and Claire went to work in the dark.

```
MASSIEKUR:        U THERE?
SEXYSPORTSBABE:   ALWAYS
MASSIEKUR:        HOMEWORK?
SEXYSPORTSBABE:   GLAMBITION. G 2 GET AN A
MASSIEKUR:        WHAT IF U DON'T GET 1?
SEXYSPORTSBABE:   U DON'T WANT 2 KNOW
MASSIEKUR:        PARENTS?
SEXYSPORTSBABE:   EVERYTHING
MASSIEKUR:        ??????
SEXYSPORTSBABE:   FORGET IT
```

MASSIEKUR:	NO, TELL ME
SEXYSPORTSBABE:	IT'S NOTHING

Todd whistled softly. Claire had four minutes left to pull a confession out of Kristen.

MASSIEKUR:	SECRET 4 A SECRET?
SEXYSPORTSBABE:	NO
MASSIEKUR:	COME ON, I HAVE SOMETHING THAT I HAVEN'T TOLD ANYONE
SEXYSPORTSBABE:	SWEAR?
MASSIEKUR:	SWEAR
SEXYSPORTSBABE:	K, U 1st
MASSIEKUR:	U KNOW HOW I'VE BEEN HANG-ING OUT WITH C.A. EVERY WEEKEND
SEXYSPORTSBABE:	UH, YEAH, I'VE NOTICED
MASSIEKUR:	LOL
	LAYNE HAS BEEN WITH US EVERY TIME
SEXYSPORTSBABE:	OMG
MASSIEKUR:	I'VE ALSO TAKEN HER FOR MANI/PEDIS AND FRO YO AFTER SCHOOL.
	I ACTUALLY LIKE HER
SEXYSPORTSBABE:	OMG X2
MASSIEKUR:	YOUR TURN
SEXYSPORTSBABE:	K BUT YOU CAN'T TELL

	U KNOW HOW I'M ALWAYS
	WORRIED ABOUT MY GRADES?
	IT'S NOT JUST CUZ I
	HAVE STRICT PARENTS. IT'S
	BECAUSE I HAVE POOR PARENTS.
	I'M ON SCHOLARSHIP AT OCD
MASSIEKUR:	OMG X3.
	I THOUGHT YOUR DAD WAS A
	RICH ART DEALER
SEXYSPORTSBABE:	WAS
MASSIEKUR:	BUT YOU LIVE IN THE MONTDOR
	BUILDING!
SEXYSPORTSBABE:	APT. BUILDING NEXT DOOR.
	SHHHHHHH.
	YOU BETTER NOT TELL! NOT
	EVEN FOR GOSSIP POINTS. K?

Todd give his final warning whistle. Claire's time was up.

| MASSIEKUR: | G2G |

MASSIEKUR HAS SIGNED OFF 8:30 P.M.

Claire knew her abrupt sign-off would rattle Kristen's nerves and make her regret sharing the secret.

"She's probably freaking out right now," Todd said. "Wondering if by this time tomorrow the whole school will know she's a poser."

His short legs raced to keep up with Claire as they scurried across the yard.

"I know," Claire said. She tried to smile but then her head started to pound. She reached for her old bracelets; playing with them had always calmed her nerves. *Huh?* She looked down at her wrist and remembered she'd cut them off.

It was starting to get chilly during the nightly walks Massie took with Bean and her father. Massie didn't mind the cool air so much because it just gave her an excuse to accessorize with scarves and hats. But Bean couldn't stand it.

She shivered in Massie's arms even though they were back inside and she was bundled up in a gray cashmere sweater and down-filled doggie booties. Massie sat on her bed and untied the laces for Bean while she finished up the conversation she was having with her father.

"Dad," Massie said. She was struggling to get Bean's last bootie off while the dog squirmed to get away. "When I ask you how I can become the next big makeup mogul, you shouldn't tell me to marry the CEO of Revlon." She giggled out of love and frustration. "What if I was the kind of daughter that took you seriously?"

"Then you wouldn't be my daughter," William said. He leaned over and kissed Massie on the forehead. He must have sensed from her pout that she wouldn't be satisfied until she got a real answer. "Okay, you want real advice?" he asked. "Find out what type of makeup the girls at your school like to use the most, whether it's lipstick or eye stuff or whatever, and then buy it wholesale."

"How is *that* going to help me become wildly popular?" Massie asked.

"Oh, is *that* the motivation?" William asked. "Sweetie, I may be a successful businessman, but I was never an expert on popularity."

"I should have known." A playful smile formed across Massie's face.

"What do you mean?" William said. He tried to sound offended.

"Wasn't Jay Lyons one of your best friends?" Massie said.

"Bean," William said. "Your mommy is evil." He rubbed the dog's tiny head and kissed Massie good night one more time before leaving.

Bean was still shivering, so Massie turned on her hair dryer and blasted her with hot air.

She reached into her dresser drawer and pulled out a baby blue cashmere blanket with a white fire hydrant sewed on the front. She wrapped Bean up like a newborn and held the shivering puppy close to her heart.

She heard a bell ding. It took a second for her to place it.

With her dog in one hand and her mouse in the other, Massie checked to see who was IM-ing her. She smoothed her hair just in case it was Chris Abeley.

SEXYSPORTSBABE: PLEASE DON'T TELL ANYONE!!!!!!!

MASSIEKUR: HUH?
SEXYSPORTSBABE: I'M SERIOUS!
MASSIEKUR: I HAVE NO IDEA WHAT
                  YOU'RE TALKING ABOUT
SEXYSPORTSBABE: THANKS ☺

"Where's Claire?" Alicia asked Massie. They were getting changed for tennis. They'd all chosen it as their sports elective because swimming dried out their hair, yoga was boring, and Tae Bo was so last year.

"How am I supposed to know?" Massie snapped.

"Isn't she your new best friend?" Alicia's voice contained a trace of bitterness.

"I'm not the one who gave her a cell phone." Massie turned toward Kristen. "Or asked her to sign up for tennis."

"She gave me her extra racket so I wouldn't have to buy one—what was I supposed to say?" Kristen screeched.

"Since when can't you afford your own racket?" Massie said.

Kristen stiffened. Her aqua blue eyes turned navy and her face became deep red.

"That's really nice, thanks a lot," Kristen said.

"Whhhat?" Massie asked.

Dylan stepped off the scale and walked over to join them.

"I'm never eating again," she said.

"Maybe you should try taking off that tent you call a skirt before you step on the scale," Massie joked. "That thing probably weighs fifteen pounds."

"But that's light compared to my fat legs, right, Massie?" Dylan said.

Massie laughed. She thought Dylan was fooling around but realized she wasn't once the skirt was airborne and heading toward her head.

"Who *are* you people and what did you do with my friends?" Massie said.

"You mean Claire, Chris, and LAYNE!" Kristen yelled. She slammed her locker shut, grabbed her tennis racket, and ran out of the locker room. Dylan took off next and then Alicia.

For the second time in her life, Massie was left standing alone.

She took a deep breath and walked into the heated bubble that covered the tennis courts. Kristen, Alicia, Dylan, and Claire were teamed up for doubles and Massie was left to find her own partners.

She felt like everyone was watching her, waiting to see what she would do next.

"How cute are your sneakers?" she said to Saylene Homer. "I can't believe you found rhinestone-covered tennis shoes."

"Thanks, Massie, I made them myself." Saylene licked her thumb and reached down to polish one of the pink stones.

Behind her back, Massie referred to her as Homer Erectus because she had perfect posture thanks to a lifetime of ballet lessons. She wore her super-long brown hair in an irritatingly high pony and only took it down for birthday parties and dances. But because of the circumstances she would have to do.

"You're so lucky," Massie said.

"I am?" Saylene sounded confused. "Why?"

"Well, not only do you have the best hair in the entire school but now you're one of the best tennis players too," Massie said. "You must have played a lot over the summer."

"Not really, no," Saylene said. "Maybe it's the shoes."

Massie offered up her best fake laugh. "Maybe," she said. "Wanna partner up? I would love to play with someone who's better than me—it's good practice."

Saylene searched for her usual partners. They were on the next court, bouncing balls on their rackets, waiting for her to join them.

"Uuuhhhh," Saylene stalled. She looked over her shoulder. "I guess it'll be okay." She noticed her friends were getting ready to start without her.

"Sure," she said.

Saylene and Massie also partnered up for lunch because they had both been exiled from their usual groups. Massie spent the rest of her day campaigning for new friends. She congratulated Suze Gellert for using up ten minutes of class time to argue with the math teacher over an answer (even though she ended up being wrong). She promised Denver Gold a burned CD by the end of the week and shared headphones with Aimee Colt so they could both listen to Massie's iPod at the same time. She felt like a politician desperate for votes. The only thing missing was a baby for her to kiss and a photographer to capture it.

She knew she could get through the year with these people

if she had to. They would eat lunch together, go to movies, and maybe even shop, but it wouldn't be the same. She already hated how her voice sounded when she talked to them. It seemed loud and foreign. Now that she was on her own, she became overly aware of everything she did.

Did Aimee think my music was cheesy? Did Saylene think I should have picked the table by the wall instead of the one by the window? Does Suze think my laugh sounds nasal?

She was out of her usual comfort zone and everything felt weird. It was the same feeling she got when she slept at someone's house and had to wear their clothes home the next day. Nothing felt familiar. She missed how reassured she felt with Alicia, Kristen, and Dylan. Over the last three years they had become her sisters. If they stopped being part of her everyday life, she knew she would go back to the way she felt before she met them. Like an only child.

Massie saw the new foursome pass her in the halls. They'd been best friends only a few days ago, but now they wouldn't even look at her. How quickly things changed. She knew their sudden outburst of laughter was fake and brought on for the sole purpose of making Massie think she was missing out on something great. After all, she was the one who taught them that trick. Instead of fighting back with the same strategy, she tried a new one.

Massie made sure to lean close to Saylene while they walked so it looked like she hung on the girl's every word. Why not let her ex-friends think she and Homer Erectus had become wildly close since third period? Massie figured this would make them crazy with jealousy. But if it did, they didn't show it.

Massie waited for them after school until 3:50 P.M., but they never showed up.

"Where is everyone?" Isaac asked when he saw Massie walk toward the car alone.

"Detention," Massie answered. "Alicia's driver is going to pick them up. We can go."

The ride home was silent. Along the way they drove right past Kristen, Alicia, Dylan, and *Claire.* The foursome walked down Briar Patch Lane barefoot holding their high-heeled shoes in their hands. They looked like they were taking a carefree stroll on the beach.

Massie slid down on the leather seat to keep from being spotted. She felt Isaac's eyes on her and was grateful that he let the moment pass without asking for an explanation.

Once the car stopped in front of the estate, Isaac unlocked the doors and Massie ran straight up to her bedroom without thanking him for the ride. She logged on to her computer, hoping one of her friends would be online, but they weren't. They were probably still walking home. She speed-dialed every one of them, but no one would pick up. She even started to dial Claire's number but stopped after three digits—she wasn't *that* desperate.

She had three new e-mails. One was from info@purple skirt.com, one was from DailyCandy, and the other was from Chris Abeley. She clicked on his name and felt her heart speed up as she waited that endless half second for the message to appear.

M,
   HOW'S IT GOING? IS EVERYTHING OKAY WITH YOU AND LAYNE? SHE SEEMS UPSET.
   BTW—I CAN'T RIDE AGAIN FOR A COUPLE OF WEEKS. THINGS ARE GETTING REALLY BUSY.
                       CHRIS

All she needed now was for her parents to tell her they were moving to Europe without her and the day would be complete.

Finally a familiar ping shot through her speakers. SexySportsBabe had sent her a message.

SEXYSPORTSBABE:	JUST 2 LET U KNOW, I HAVE A RIDE FOR TOMORROW. DON'T PICK ME UP
MASSIEKUR:	WHAT IS GOING ON?????
SEXYSPORTSBABE:	STOP ACTING ALL INNOCENT. I TRUSTED YOU. YOU SAID YOU WOULD KEEP OUR SECRET!!!
MASSIEKUR:	WHAT SECRET? I HONESTLY HAVE NO IDEA WHAT YOU'RE TALKING ABOUT!

Massie dialed Kristen's cell phone.

"You have three minutes," Kristen said.

Massie knew she was serious and was grateful she'd answered the phone.

"Kristen, for the last time, I have no idea what secret you're talking about," Massie said.

"You told me about being friends with Layne and I—"

"I never told you I was friends with Layne," Massie snapped. "Who said I was friends with Layne?"

Kristen started talking like a detective. "Last night at 8:26 P.M., you told me that you were hanging out with Layne and then I told you—"

"Wait—," Massie said.

"*Stop cutting me off!*" Kristen said.

"But I was out walking Bean at 8:26 P.M. When I sent you that message last night telling you I didn't know what you were talking about, I was serious," Massie said.

She lifted Bean off her lap and gently placed her on the floor. She needed to pace.

"Then how do you explain the IMs that were coming from *your* computer?" Kristen asked.

"I have no idea," Massie said.

"Why should I believe you?" Kristen asked.

"Because if I was lying, you know I'd have come up with a way better excuse than that," Massie said.

Kristen's face slowly broke into a smile and then she let out a small laugh. "That's true."

Claire and Alicia were on the last legs of their long walk home. Alicia was talking about *something* that had happened during last period. It had to do with a bottle of rubber cement and Jaden Hiltz's rabbit-foot key chain, but that was all Claire heard. She had been too busy thinking about her new "friends."

Claire knew the girls were only being nice to her for two reasons: (1) Because she had tricked them into thinking Massie liked her; and (2) They'd stopped liking Massie.

But Claire didn't care, not much anyway. Besides, anything was better than being abused, right? She wanted to hold on to this false sense of security for as long as possible. Even if she was having trouble sleeping at night, even if her stomach hurt

They had parted ways with Kristen and Dylan four blocks back and were just around the corner from Alicia's.

"Thank God we made it," Alicia said. She was dragging her Prada messenger bag along the ground.

"We must have walked at least six miles," Claire said.

"It was worth it. The last thing I wanted to do was share a car with Massie Blecchh," Alicia said.

"I know." Claire rolled her eyes. "I can't believe I have to go back to that house right now." She was doing everything she could to keep the girls in their anti-Massie phase.

"You don't," Alicia said. Her eyes twinkled more than usual. "Let's go buy something to wear to Dylan's birthday."

Claire didn't know how to tell Alicia that she had a total of three dollars in her bag and most of it was in change.

"I would love to, but I left my credit cards at home," Claire said.

"No prob. I'll pay," Alicia said.

"I can't let you do that," Claire said.

"Sure, you can," Alicia said. She took out five different credit cards and held them like a winning hand of poker.

Normally Claire would have spent a lot more time objecting, but she had seen Alicia pay for the other girls on several occasions and no one seemed to give it much thought. She liked that Alicia wanted to treat her. Not for the free clothes but because it meant she considered Claire a friend.

How else would she have been able to buy the Swiss-dot silk DKNY dress ($248), the Marc by Marc Jacobs leather kitten heels ($265), the BCBG beaded clutch ($108), and the hair clip ($32)? The grand total (not including tax) came to $653.00. That was exactly $53 more than she had saved up from the birthday money her grandmother sent every year.

It was dark out by the time Claire was finally dropped off by Alicia's driver. As she walked across the path to her house, she looked at Massie's window and saw her sitting alone at her computer. Claire swallowed hard.

Okay, so Massie looked sort of pathetic sitting there by

herself. But then again, Claire was the one who'd been banished to the backseat of the car and ignored in the hallways and had red paint dumped on her pants, had food dumped all over her and—worst of all—had Layne stolen away from her. So when she thought of it that way, she didn't feel like such a horrible person. *She* was the victim in all this. That meant *she* could do whatever she wanted to make herself feel better. Didn't it?

"Where have you been?" Judi asked. She was en route from the kitchen to the front hall.

Claire tossed her shopping bags in the front hall closet and managed to get the door closed before her mother appeared.

"What did you do to your hair?" Judi asked. She was looking at the awkward way Claire's bangs were pinned away from her face.

"Sorry, I ended up going to Alicia's house after school to study," Claire said. She couldn't believe she had forgotten to call home.

"I was going out of my mind with worry," she said. "I called Layne and Massie and neither one of them had any idea where you had gone. I taught you how to call home when you were five years old."

"I'm sorry, okay!" Claire shouted.

"'Sorry' doesn't change the fact that you didn't call," Judi said. "For the next two weeks I want you home straight after school."

Claire couldn't believe her bad luck. "I thought you

wanted me to make new friends! Now that I finally did, you won't let me hang out with them?"

"You're missing the point, Claire," Judi said.

But Claire didn't care about "the point." She ran up the stairs and slammed her bedroom door behind her. A framed black-and-white photograph of some lady taken next to what might have been the *Titanic* fell off her wall and crashed to the floor.

Before Claire could pick up the glass, Mr. Rivera's cell phone rang. She answered it quickly so her mother wouldn't know she had a phone.

"Claire? What's up? It's Kristen."

"My mom freaked out on me because I just got home," Claire said.

"Where were you?" Kristen asked. She sounded overly concerned.

"Shopping with Alicia, buying outfits for Dylan's party," Claire said.

"I didn't know you had a credit card. That's awesome," Kristen said. Claire thought she sounded a little jealous and knew exactly why.

"Alicia paid," Claire said.

"She did?"

"Doesn't she always. I think tomorrow I'm going to make her go back and get me the matching coat."

Claire heard the sound of someone gasping on the line and knew exactly what was going on.

"Todd, hang up!" she shouted. "Sorry 'bout that. My stupid brother was listening."

"No problem. Look, I should probably go. It's getting close to 8 P.M., which means my mother is about to cut me off. See you tomorrow?" Kristen said.

"Yup, see ya," Claire said, and then hung up.

Mr. Rivera's cell phone rang again. It was Dylan.

"I hear you bought a great outfit for my party," she said.

"Yeah, it's pretty cool. The dress is super-tight and the heels are pretty high," Claire said. "Alicia said it looked smokin' on me."

"I know, she told me," Dylan said. "She also told me you scored a few gossip points on your walk home."

Claire panicked at first, quickly shuttling through her day in fast-forward, trying to remember if she told anyone about Kristen being on scholarship.

"I did?" Claire asked.

"Yeah, you told her about Massie and Layne," Dylan said.

"Oh yeah, that's right," Claire said. "All those times Massie canceled plans with you to hang out with Chris Abeley she was also with Layne."

"Two points," Dylan said.

"They even went out after school a few times," Claire said.

"Another point," Dylan said. "How do you know?"

"Layne told me," Claire said.

Dylan was silent.

"You know, when we were hanging out," Claire said. "Before I got to know you guys."

"I can't believe Massie lied to us." Dylan sounded hurt. "Maybe I should uninvite her to my party."

"I would," Claire said. "Unless of course you want her to make you feel guilty every time you have a bite of your own birthday cake."

"You're so right!" Dylan said. "Claire, is that the only secret you know?"

"About Massie?" Claire asked.

"About anyone," Dylan asked.

Claire knew she would score double gossip points if she told Dylan about Kristen's scholarship, triple points if she mentioned Kristen was poor, and quadruple if she revealed Kristen's real address.

"Yeah," Claire said.

"Yeah, what?" Dylan asked.

"Yeah, that's it," Claire said.

"'Kay, thanks. Bye," Dylan said. *Click.*

"Bye." Alicia giggled. *Click.*

"See ya," Kristen said. *Click.*

"Nighty night," Massie said. *Click.*

Claire's mouth opened and then closed and then opened again, but nothing came out. She felt dizzy and briefly wondered if she was going to faint because her heart was beating so quickly.

How would she fix this? Even her parents were mad at her. How could she be so stupid? She was on a cell phone. A *cell phone!* It was impossible for her brother to have been on the line—she was the victim of a five-way!

When the dog bites
When the bee stings
When I'm feeling sad
I simply remember my favorite things
And then I don't feel . . . so bad. . . .

Claire sang the chorus over and over again. After the third time she decided that it was time to start looking for a new song. This one wasn't working anymore.

The girls stood barefoot on the smooth marble countertop in Alicia's kitchen. They were reaching to unhook the shiny copper pots and pans that hung on the racks above them. To their right were two shiny Sub-Zero refrigerators and to their left were two shiny chrome sinks.

"Hurry," Alicia whispered. "My mom will freak if she sees us standing up here without socks on."

Once they got everything they needed, they sat down and took a break.

Massie disappeared into the hallway and came back with a navy blue L. L. Bean bag. She reached in, pulled out a gift-wrapped box, and handed it to Kristen.

"What is this?" Kristen asked. She tore the bow with her teeth, trying to get it open.

"Easy," Massie said. "Wait until everyone has theirs so you can all open them together."

As soon as Massie handed out the last box, she gave the order.

"One, two, three, open them!" she said.

"Ehmagod."

"I love it!"

"Amazing!"

"I got one for myself too." Massie took her white satin robe out of the tissue paper and held it out in front of her. It said *Glambition* across the back in purple script and *Massie* on the front, in the top left corner. Each robe was personalized.

"I figured they're so much cuter than lab coats," Massie said.

"Totally!" Alicia said.

They slid into their robes and rolled up their sleeves.

"I love our company," Kristen said. "Now all we have to do is make the stuff."

The field trip into Manhattan was on Monday, leaving them only two and a half days to create their entire inventory.

Alicia lined up a long row of clear round pill holders that she bought at the drugstore. Dylan rummaged through the pots and pans with no regard for the loud clanging sounds she was creating.

"Quiet down, you'll wake the neighbors," Alicia said. It was a joke, of course—the Riveras had so much land, the nearest neighbors were at least a quarter mile away.

"Speaking of neighbors, I wonder what Claire is doing right now?" Massie asked.

"Maybe she moved back to O-Town," Alicia suggested.

"She must have been really freaked out by our call," Massie said. "If that was me, I'd probably switch schools."

"Hopefully she will," Dylan said.

"I can't believe she had you guys going for so long on IM," Massie said.

"I can't believe she snuck in your room every night without you catching her," Kristen said.

"I know, it's pretty impressive." Massie gave a distant smile. She looked up and saw her friends looking at her like she was crazy. "I mean, I'm just surprised she even came up with the idea. You know, 'cause she seems like such a goody-goody. It seems like something we would do."

"Can we please get started?" Kristen said. She shook the piece of paper she had been holding in the air.

"Just tell me what we need and I'll grab it," Dylan said. She was standing in front of the open cupboards, ready to pull out whatever ingredients Kristen was about to read off.

3 oz. almond oil

½ oz. beeswax

2 Tbsp. honey

3–4 drops peppermint oil

"Where did you get the recipe?" Dylan asked.

"Online," Kristen said.

Kristen read the directions out loud so Massie could follow them.

"Melt the almond oil and beeswax in a small saucepan over low heat until wax is soft," she read.

Once that step was complete, Alicia took over.

"Remove from heat. Add honey and blend mixture thoroughly," Kristen read.

Alicia handed the wooden spoon to Dylan. Kristen continued.

"Stir the mixture occasionally as it cools to prevent separation. It should have the consistency of petroleum jelly when ready."

When she finished reading, she took the spoon from Dylan and gave it a stir. It was important to Kristen that everyone take part in creating the potion.

Kristen dipped her finger in the gloss as it cooled. She brought it to her mouth and stuck her tongue out to have a taste.

"Eeewww." Alicia wrinkled her nose.

"What? All the ingredients are edible," Kristen said.

"Lemme try." Dylan scraped her finger across the side of the pot and licked it. "It's not bad."

"Want some?" Dylan held the pot out to Massie.

"No thanks, I'm allergic to nuts," she said.

"Why didn't you tell me?" Kristen said. "I would have picked a different recipe."

"I already *have* lip gloss," Massie said. "I'm doing this for the cachet!"

The girls laughed at Massie's attempt to sound like a businesswoman. But the smile on her face was there for a different reason. She was happy she had her friends back.

Claire stumbled past the row of family photos that leaned against a wall in her parents' room and threw herself on their wrought iron four-poster bed. She was relieved to see that the pictures still hadn't been hung up. If the house wasn't fully set up yet, maybe that meant they weren't staying long. Maybe they'd get to move out sooner than she thought.

She wrapped herself in the frilly country-style comforter and curled up in a tight ball.

"Mom, I don't feel well," she said.

Judi was in the bathroom, wearing only her bra and panty hose, blow-drying her hair. Her tiny portable TV was propped up on a stack of self-help books by the sink. She was a slave to *The Daily Grind.* Claire had yet to tell her mother that she knew Merri-Lee Marvil's daughter because then she'd have to explain why she couldn't introduce her.

Sorry, Mom, I know you lined up for nineteen hours to see The Daily Grind *when it shot a week's worth of shows from Disney World. . . . Yes, I know you are a member of Merri-Lee Marvil's Recipe of the Month Club, but that doesn't change the fact that her daughter hates me. . . . I'm not sure why. . . . It started the minute she laid eyes on me. . . . No, there's no chance we'll become friends. . . .*

Actually there was a chance, but I blew it by talking behind her back and getting caught. . . . Mom . . . where are you going? Why are you packing my bags? Why are you throwing me out of your house? But I don't want to live with another family. . . .

"Maaaaa." Claire rolled from one side to the other and wrapped her arms around her kneecaps for effect.

"What is it?" Judi asked. "Are you sick?"

"I think I have food poisoning," Claire said.

Finally Judi tore herself away from the TV and creaked across the hardwood floor to the bed.

"How is that possible? You didn't even touch your dinner last night."

"Maybe it's the flu. I should probably stay home," Claire offered.

"Then we're going to the doctor," Judi said.

"I'm sure I'll be okay in a few hours." Claire whimpered. "Can't we just wait a bit?"

"Maybe you should tell me what's really going on," Judi said. "I'll drive you to school today and we can talk in the car."

Claire stuffed her cell phone in her pajamas and ran up the stairs to the attic. She climbed over a pink tricycle, two mountain bikes, a Razor scooter, several pair of roller blades, tennis rackets, a small motorized Jeep, and boxes labeled *Beanie Babies, Barbies,* and *Shoelace collection.* It was like a burial ground for Massie's dead toys. She finally made it to the diamond-shaped window that overlooked the Blocks' driveway. Isaac was scraping something off the roof of the car (bird poo?) and Massie was leaning against the rear door talking on her Motorola. She never liked to wait inside the car.

Claire called Isaac and watched him struggle to get his phone out of the inside pocket of his blazer.

"Hello, Claire. Are you on your way down?"

"Actually, I'm calling to let you know that I'm getting a ride from my mother today." Claire saw Massie hang up her phone and walk over to Isaac. "We are going to look at a few houses today on our way to school."

"You're not moving out already, are you?" Isaac asked.

"Maybe," Claire said.

After they hung up the phone, Claire saw Isaac explain the call to Massie. When Isaac returned to his scraping, Massie turned to face the guest house. She ran her fingers through her hair and almost looked troubled by the news.

Judi's pep talk was pretty standard. Filled with all the sorts of things mothers are taught to tell their daughters in situations such as this: "Those girls aren't worth getting sick over," and, "It won't be long before they realize what they're missing," and, "When I was your age, a similar thing happened to me," but it wasn't enough. Especially once Claire was dropped off in front of a school bus filled with her classmates, who were anxiously awaiting her arrival. Not because they liked her but because they couldn't leave on their field trip without her. Vincent, the art teacher and chaperone for the day, wouldn't let them.

Claire quickly kissed her mother goodbye and ran out of their rental car.

"I was just about to call ABC studios and ask if they wouldn't mind taping *All My Children* a few hours later today because Claire Lyons was running a little late," he said. "But if you can find a seat in the next *second,* I'll refrain."

Claire's eyes went straight to Massie, Kristen, Alicia, and Dylan, who were sitting across the last row of the bus—the only seat that could hold all four of them.

Directly in front of them were available spaces that no one dared fill without an invitation. And just to make sure, the girls had tossed their jackets, bags, and notebooks on them.

"Alicia, maybe you can *buy* Claire someone to sit beside," Dylan said loud enough for everyone to hear.

Their high fives sounded more like gunshots to Claire. A few of the other girls on the bus snickered, which made Claire even more upset because they didn't even get the joke.

"Claire, I'd offer you a seat back here if Dylan's fat legs didn't take up so much room," Alicia said.

More gunshots.

Claire had no idea how she was going to make it through the day. She had no one on her side.

"Claire. Sit. Now," Vincent barked.

The only seat that wasn't off-limits was beside Layne. Meena and Heather weren't anywhere near her, and Claire figured they were mad at her for blowing them off for Massie. It seemed like everyone's world had returned to normal except her own and Layne's.

Claire was happy to see that Layne's fingernails were no longer painted "Massie Pink." They were back to green and her thumbs blue. Her hair was in two pigtails and she was wearing flip-flops with leg warmers. Layne was finally acting like her old self again. Unfortunately, that also meant her oatmeal was making the trip into Manhattan with them.

Claire managed to avoid eye contact with Layne when she sat down. She settled into the aisle seat and prayed for an alien abduction. But the screech of the releasing brakes and the phlegmy sound of the revving engine told Claire that she wasn't going to be rescued anytime soon.

The instant the bus made its wide turn out of the school parking lot, the thirty girls on board came to life. The pop divas blasted remixes from a boom box, the butt kissers swarmed Vincent to ask what school was like when he was a kid, and the driver told war stories to the suckers who'd gotten stuck sitting behind him. Only the back of the bus was quiet, because Massie, Kristen, Alicia, and Dylan were whispering.

"Can I have everyone's attention, please," Massie shouted. She waited patiently for the noise to die down.

Claire faced forward and ignored her.

"Thank you, Kara," she said to one of the pop divas after she lowered her music. "I would like to introduce you to a new line of cosmetics called Glambition. Here to tell you more about it is Glambition's president, Kristen Gregory." Massie started clapping and everyone followed.

Claire couldn't resist any longer. She twisted her neck around so her left cheek was pressed against the prickly cloth on the seat and her right eye was free to examine what was going on.

All four girls were dressed in their matching white satin robes. They sat in their seats with their legs crossed and heads tilted up toward Kristen, who stood up and addressed the bus.

"Glambition is a new brand of beauty products made from one hundred percent natural ingredients." Claire thought she sounded like she was a washed-up actress on an infomercial. "Over the next few weeks we will introduce you to our complete line of creams, scrubs, body glitters, and cheek tints, but today we are launching our clear lip gloss. It comes in four flavors: Massie, Dylan, Alicia, and Kristen," Kristen said. "Since you're our first customers, we're offering this very special product to you for the low price of five-fifty for one and ten dollars for two."

Massie jumped up and added, "Not only does it look good but the Briarwood boys love the taste, if you know what I mean," she said.

Vincent's jaw dropped and he placed his sweaty palm on one of the windows to keep himself from falling as he stood up to shake his "warning finger" at Massie.

"Lies!" Layne shouted softly so only Claire could hear. "The Briarwood boy she's talking about is madly in love with *his girlfriend*."

But Massie's audience clearly had no idea. They unleashed a fury of applause, "whoo-hooos," and "yahs" to show that they not only approved of Massie's promiscuity but that they liked to kiss boys too.

"What. Ever," Claire said. She knocked her head against the back of her seat.

Hands started waving in the air, numbers were being shouted out, and everyone was fighting to get Kristen's attention.

"How New York Stock Exchange is *this?*" Massie started walking the aisles handing out gloss and collecting money. Kristen, Alicia, and Dylan did the same.

"I'll take one," Layne said. "Why not, right?"

Claire saw Layne avoid her disapproving eyes as she handed a ten-dollar bill to Alicia.

"We only have mint, cherry, vanilla, and raspberry today, no oatmeal, sorry," Alicia said. "Maybe next week."

Then Alicia looked at Claire and in her loudest voice said, "Oh, and Claire, we have a new line coming out next month called TWO-FACED—you should probably wait for that one, it's more your style."

Claire peeled a strip of rubber off the side of her sneaker. She thought about telling them they should make a new line called SHALLOW GIRLS, but decided against it.

"Claire, I'm sorry I ditched you for Massie," Layne said.

The words came out so quickly, it took Claire a second to understand what she had said.

"No, you're not," Claire said. "You're just sorry because Massie ditched you."

"I could say the same thing about you," Layne fired back.

"Only I never ditched you, Layne," Claire said.

"What about the night you had to 'babysit' your 'sick' brother?"

Claire felt her face burn.

"How did you know?" Claire said.

"Are you forgetting I was 'friends' with Massie?"

"Why didn't you say something sooner?"

"Well," said Layne. And then she paused for a long time and took a deep breath. "Because I would have done the same thing." She exhaled. "But not anymore, I swear." She held out her pinky finger and waited patiently for Claire's. But Claire held back.

"Come on, I'll forgive if you will," Layne said.

Claire looked past Layne's tiny green nail and straight into her eyes. She held her stare for a second and when she felt her own face soften, she shifted her gaze to her backpack, hoping to appear tough for a few seconds longer.

She unzipped and zipped five different zippers before she found the pocket that held her camera. She pressed a button and shuttled through the pictures she had taken over the last few days.

"I will forgive you, and I will shake that pinky of yours, if you can explain *this*." She held the camera straight out in front of them so they could both look at the tiny screen together.

The first picture was of Layne talking to Massie in a deserted hallway. She was wearing a white knee-length skirt, a lime green Izod, and white pointy flats. Massie was wearing the exact same outfit, except her shirt was navy.

"What's up, Mini Me?" Claire joked.

Layne cracked up and turned red.

"Okay, I admit it, I was a total Massie wannabe for a few weeks," Layne said. "But I'm back!" She tugged on her purple leg warmers just to prove it.

"At least you lasted a few weeks. That's more than most people on this bus," Claire said.

They both laughed and locked pinkies.

"Friends?" Layne asked.

"Friends," Claire answered.

"I'm sorry to announce that we have completely sold out of Massie, Alicia, Kristen, and Dylan," Kristen announced. "But if you're interested in getting our newsletter by e-mail, Dylan will be passing around a sign-up book."

Kristen took a wad of cash to the back of bus and counted it in a closed huddle with the rest of her partners. She paid them each twenty dollars for their work and tucked the rest away in her Miu Miu fanny belt.

Meanwhile Claire and Layne forced their faces to fit inside the crack between their two seats so they could laugh at the sea of greasy, gloopy lips behind them.

"Test test," Vincent called over the loudspeaker. He stood at the front of the bus, twirling the thick coiled black cord that hung from the bottom of the mike. His thumb held down the button on the side so his voice would be amplified.

"STUDENTS." His voice nearly shattered the eardrums of every girl on the bus. He tweaked the volume dial and tried again.

"Students," he said softly. "That's better."

"Dork," a muffled voice shouted from the back of the bus. A sprinkle of giggles followed.

Vincent pulled his goatee and curled his lips inward so it looked like he had no mouth. He waited patiently for the disruption to cease.

"As some of you may already know, we have been granted permission to visit the set of *All My Children* today because I happen to be very special friends with one of the actors. So I expect all of you to be on your best behav—"

"It burnzzz," someone hollered from the middle of the bus. "My lips are on fire!!!"

Amanda Levine stood up and fanned her face as if it had been torched.

"Mine too," Noel Durkins wailed. She turned to face the back of the bus. Her eyes bulged when she heard the gasps that came after everyone saw her.

"What?" she shouted. "Whhhattt?"

"Oh my God, her lips look like they got breast implants," Layne said to Claire.

"Big time," Claire said.

Massie pushed her way through the hysteria and grabbed the microphone out of Vincent's hand.

"Calm down." Massie plastered a big, bright smile on her face. "It's just the natural emollients working their way through your lips. It's nothing to worry about."

"I have it too," Debby Weezer yelled.

"Debby, call your mother's plastic surgeon," Michelle Powers said.

"For the hundredth time, my mom doesn't *have* a plastic surgeon, Michelle!" Debby snapped.

Massie addressed the girls again. "Just out of curiosity, how many of you are allergic to peanuts or nuts of any kind? I'm looking for a show of hands here."

At least ten hands shot into the air.

"Thank you," Massie said. She handed the mike back to Vincent and marched to the back of the bus.

"We want our money back," Carrie Drebin shouted.

"Yeah!" Debby said.

"I just want my lips back," Carolyn Rothstein said.

"Mine are so itchy," Carly Cooper said.

Vincent flicked on the mike. "Everyone, *please relax,*" he said.

No one did. Kristen's blubbering could be heard all the way in the front of the bus. It mingled with the existing sobs and created a symphony of hysteria.

"I'm going to f-f-f-faaaaail," she bawled.

Vincent whispered something in the driver's hairy ear and the bus pulled over at the side of the highway.

"*Enough* screaming, you harpies!" Vincent said. "I can't hear myself think."

His lack of anything helpful to say just made everyone panic even more.

Layne and Claire were the only ones on the entire bus who managed to stay calm.

"You're vibrating." Layne pointed to Claire's backpack.

"What?" Claire asked. "Oh, it must be my phone."

Layne crinkled her eyebrows when Claire took the humming silver cell phone from her bag.

"Since when did you get a—?" Layne was cut off.

"Long story," Claire said. She didn't recognize the incoming number, so she hung up.

It buzzed again.

"Who *is* it?" Layne asked.

"I don't know," Claire said before hanging up a second time. "Probably a prank."

The third time the phone beeped, indicating that Claire had a text message. Claire checked the screen.

914-555-8055:	OATMEAL.
CLAIRE:	LEAVE LAYNE ALONE!!!
914-555-8055:	U DON'T GET IT.
	HER OATMEAL WILL HELP.
	GOOD 4 RASHES, ETC. . . .
	READ IT IN COSMO ☺

"Layne, do you have any more oatmeal?" Claire asked. She was already searching through Layne's bag.

Layne grabbed the bag back from Claire. "Why is everyone so obsessed with my oatmeal? God! They've got to get some new material. This is getting sooo boring."

"No, Layne, your oatmeal will help," Claire said. "I remember my mother soaking me in an oatmeal bath when I had poison ivy. It totally works."

She tried to pry it from Layne's grip, but it wasn't easy.

"Why should I help *them* when all they do is make fun of me?" Layne asked.

"This is why." Claire grabbed Layne's thermos and pushed her way through the pack of screaming girls who were fighting over Carly's hand mirror.

"I can help," Claire shouted as loud as she could. She held the thermos above her head like Moses holding the Ten Commandments.

"Help me," Noel shouted.

"No, me, look at my face!" Michelle said.

"It will cost you two dollars," Claire said.

Layne looked tickled by the announcement. She gave Claire a thumbs-up from her seat.

The angry mob turned toward Kristen and demanded their money back.

"What's in there?" Vincent asked.

"Oatmeal," Claire said with a proud smile.

"I refuse to let you charge these suffering girls for hot cereal," he said.

"Why? You're the one who let them pay for rotten lip gloss," Layne jumped in.

"Here, take five dollars." Carly was waving her cash in the air. "Just hurry!"

Claire looked at Vincent. He waved her off as if to say, *Leave me out of it*, and sat down in the empty seat behind the driver.

Claire started doling out the rations and Layne followed her, collecting the cash.

One by one, the girls dug their hands into the white plastic thermos cup and scooped out their share of oatmeal. They smeared it on their mouths with no concern for the raisins that slid down their chins.

The bus was quiet once the oatmeal had been applied. They just sat in their seats, covered in gooey globs, silently staring straight ahead. No one wanted to open their mouths for fear of swallowing some of it by mistake.

The only sound that could be heard was Kristen, weeping in the back. Everyone thought she was being kind of a drama queen about it. Only Claire knew how badly Kristen really needed an A . . . and the money.

The bus turned around and headed north on the Saw Mill River Parkway. The *All My Children* trip was turning into a visit to the Westchester Medical Center.

The girls with the swollen faces poured off the bus and ran toward the entrance while Vincent followed, begging them to slow down. The few normal faces split up. Massie led half of them to the vending machine while the other half lingered outside the bus.

"Thank you," Kristen said. Claire was bent over tying her shoe and didn't realize she was being spoken to.

"Seriously, I mean it. Thanks," Kristen said again.

Claire's body hung over her shoe, but her head snapped up to see if this person was actually talking to *her.*

"Don't thank me, it was Layne's oatmeal," Claire said.

"No, not for that, for the other thing." Kristen looked around to make sure no one was listening.

"Ohhh, that. Well, I promised, didn't I?" She liked the way those words sounded, sincere and honest. She almost had forgotten that part of her existed.

"I'm actually happy it was you I told and not Massie." Kristen looked around one more time before continuing. "There, now that's two secrets you have to keep."

"No problem. By the way, I'm sorry about your company," Claire said. She meant it.

But Kristen didn't answer. Instead she turned and walked away to look for her friends.

┌───┐
│   │
│   THE RANGE ROVER   │
│   FIRST-CLASS SECTION   │
│   │
│   8:10 A.M.   │
│   October 1st   │
│   │
└───┘

"Look, Dylan, your mom is showing pictures from your birthday party," Massie said. She cranked up the volume on the TV and closed the car windows so she wouldn't miss a word. The girls leaned back against the seats and gazed up at the screen.

"How much do I love Justin Timberlake?" Merri-Lee said as she held out a photograph of the musician stuffing a piece of Dylan's birthday cake in his mouth. The camera zoomed in.

"Where are the pictures of *us,* Mom?" Dylan asked the TV.

"And here is the birthday girl, my daughter, Dylan. I have no idea where all of that fabulous red hair came from, because I get mine from Rena, the brilliant colorist who works at Avalon. Love you, Rena." Merri-Lee blew a kiss to the camera. "See you Thursday." The audience gave huge laughs for that one, followed by applause.

"I can't believe people think she's funny," Dylan said.

"Here she is again, dancing with her gorgeous girl-friends," she said, right on cue. "I'm telling you, they could all be models." The camera pushed in on a sultry shot of Alicia looking straight through the lens.

"Ehmagod, look how sweaty I am," Alicia shouted.

Dylan shifted in her seat. Massie knew Dylan thought

her mother gave Alicia way too many compliments on her looks. At least triple what she gave her own daughter.

Dylan's response was to gather up a thick bushel of red hair and drop it over the back of her shoulders. But her hair was so heavy, it made her ears fold over like taco shells.

Massie reached for her phone.

MASSIE: EARZ
KRISTEN: I. C.
ALICIA: W8ER THERE'S A HAIR IN MY TACO
KRISTEN: I siiiiiiiii
MASSIE: WHAT? I CAN'T EAR U!

It wasn't until they all burst out laughing that Dylan realized she was being made fun of.

Her eyes shifted from Alicia to Massie to Kristen. "What?" she asked. She noticed their attempts to hide their phones and went straight for Alicia's because she was the weakest and the easiest to tackle. "What did you write?"

Dylan scrolled through to see what they had written.

"Oh yeah?" Dylan laughed. "At least I didn't look deep fried on national television," she said to Alicia.

Even Isaac laughed at that one.

Massie felt an unexpected wave of warmth roll through her stomach. She called it the "the feeling." It happened whenever she had a genuine "I love these people" sensation. It didn't come around too often, but when it did, it was so powerful it could actually make her tear up.

As if the moment had been too good to be true, Massie checked over her shoulder, just to make sure Claire wasn't in the backseat, breathing down her neck and listening to everything she was saying. She wasn't. Things were finally back to normal and everyone was exactly where they belonged.

"Please tell me you are going to the Blocks' OCD benefit auction Friday night," Claire said to Layne. They were sitting in the back of Mr. Abeley's freezing cold Jaguar with their bare feet pressed up against the gusty air conditioner vents, trying to see who could hold out the longest without moving. They never played for a prize, just glory.

"We go every year," Layne said. "If we can steer clear of Massie and her friends, we may actually have a good time."

Claire leaned into the front seat of the car and craned her neck around so she faced the passenger seat.

"Chris, are you and Fawn going?" she asked. She popped a gummy bear in her mouth and held the bag open for Layne.

"We wouldn't miss it for the world," Chris said.

Claire mouthed, "Yes!" to Layne. She couldn't wait for Massie to meet Fawn.

Chris turned toward Claire. She noticed his eyes were the exact same color as his royal blue Polo shirt.

"The place is set up like a five-star food court. They have chefs serving every type of dish you could ever imagine."

But he could have been quoting a computer manual and Claire would have been glued. If she had to say one nice thing about Massie, it would be that she had great taste in guys.

"But the best part is watching Mr. Block get drunk and make an ass out of himself," he said.

"Chris!" Mr. Abeley snapped.

"What, Dad? You know it's true." Chris laughed. "Last year he juggled, *and dropped*, three bottles of champagne." He turned toward the backseat to face his sister. "Layne, I worship you for e-mailing me the video at boarding school. I must have forwarded it to every guy at Kingsley."

Claire laughed. She was excited to go to the party, especially now that she had someone on her side.

"Feel like moving your feet yet?" Layne asked. She was baiting Claire, hoping for a victory after her two-day losing streak. "I think your toes are turning blue."

"Don't worry about me, I can handle it," Claire said, knowing a few weeks ago she would have already surrendered.

Girls covered the stone steps in front of OCD, waiting to get picked up after school. The crisp air felt like it was trying to push the last remaining of bits of warmth out of the way so it could take over for good. And it seemed everyone was embracing the new season by wearing the latest fall fashions.

At least half the girls were wearing stiff dark denim jackets that begged to be broken in.

"Looks like there was an explosion in the Levi's factory," Kristen said.

"Seriously, doesn't anyone think for themselves anymore?" Dylan wondered.

Alicia hit Massie on the arm.

"Ow!" Massie rubbed her arm.

"Burberry poncho, no punch-backs!" Alicia cheered.

A girl shrouded in what looked like a horse blanket rolled her eyes and sped past them.

"You are so dead," Massie joked. She cracked her knuckles and tried to look tough. She did a quick scan of the outfits in the general vicinity in hopes of immediate revenge, but she was out of luck.

"You may want to wear a layer of padding to the auction

tonight," Massie warned. "My mother's friends still think Burberry is cool."

"Does anyone want to get ready at my house?" Alicia asked.

Dylan looked at Massie, waiting for her response.

"I can't," Massie said. "Chris Abeley is coming, which means I only have three hours to become a 'ten.' I'm definitely going to need my own hair dryer and stuff."

"I can't either," Dylan said.

"Kris?" Alicia asked.

"I have to get started on my extra-credit assignment," Kristen announced.

"How'd you convince your Women in the Workforce teacher to give you one?" Massie asked.

"She was so relieved that no one was seriously hurt and no parents decided to sue after the lip gloss incident that she said I could make up my own. I read ahead in my economics book and noticed chapter 11 was called "How to Declare Bankruptcy." So I e-mailed my teacher and she said that if I can figure out how to file correctly, she'll give me an A," Kristen said.

"Genius!" Massie clapped. "Don't worry, we'll find another, better way to take over the school."

"I wasn't worried about *that*." Kristen smirked.

"I know. That comment was meant for me," Massie said. She flashed her friend a big-toothy smile.

When Massie got home, the Block estate was already buzzing with excitement. Men and women from the furniture rental place were unloading long wooden tables, people from the florists were scurrying around holding giant bouquets of tulips, and caterers had taken over the kitchen. Everyone in town would be at her house by 7:30 P.M. It was a huge deal.

Massie snuck up to her bedroom and locked her door just in case her mother wanted her to do any last minute errands. She needed time to unwind and focus on getting ready.

She slid five CDs in the stereo, hit shuffle, and opened her closet door. Then she stood back, crossed her arms, and appraised her weapons, wondering which was best suited for tonight's battle: Jimmy Choo high-heel mules, Miu Miu wedges, Calvin flats, Jimmy Choo sandals, DKNY stiletto boots, or the Marc Jacobs pumps? Jimmy Choo high-heel mules, of course. It was important for Chris to see her in something sexy instead of the sporty outfits she always wore riding.

She felt a wave of resentment toward Claire shoot through her body. If she had been allowed to go on the Labor Day shopping trip, she would have had a much wider shoe selection to choose from.

After several outfit changes Massie chose a purple chiffon dress with a halter strap that tied around her neck. Simple and elegant. She made sure Bean looked just as stylish by dressing her in a white doggie button-down with gold bone buttons. She grabbed Chris's Yankees hat off her desk and sprayed Chanel No. 19 on it just so he'd have her on the brain next time he wore it.

The muffled sounds of the band playing Sinatra's "Mack

the Knife" seeped through Massie's bedroom walls, which meant the party had officially started.

"Massie?" Kendra's voice came over the intercom. "Everyone is asking where you are. Come on down."

" 'Kay," Massie called into the white box. "Let's go break some hearts, Bean."

Bean turned around in a circle and headed out the door.

Massie searched the big white tent in her backyard for her friends, but she couldn't see them. She was about to dial them up to find out where they were when she spotted Chris Abeley at the bar. She thought about waiting for the girls to arrive before she talked to him so they could see how cute they looked together, but Claire was already with him, so there was no time to waste.

Massie motioned for Bean to stay close so she wouldn't get trampled as they made their way through the thick crowd. She was grateful for the mass of people that stood between her and Chris Abeley because it kept him from noticing her heels getting stuck in the grass every time she took a step. At one point she moved forward, but her Choo stayed firmly planted in the mud. She walked the rest of the way on her tiptoes.

Massie reached down and picked Bean up in her arms so the dog could finally meet Chris Abeley. She pushed her way into his circle and was disappointed to find Bean taking a greater interest in Claire's bag of gummies than in Chris.

"This must be Bean," Chris Abeley said.

"That's right." Massie waved Bean's front paw at Chris.

"Say hello, Bean." She could smell his familiar scent of deodorant and fabric softener.

She wished they had plans to ride the next day, but they didn't.

"Layne, are you up for another riding lesson tomorrow?" Massie asked while looking at Chris.

Layne exchanged a confident look with Claire before answering.

"No, Claire and I are going to the movies." Layne dipped her hand in Claire's sweaty bag of gummies and slurped a worm into her mouth like it was a piece of spaghetti.

"Good, 'cause you sucked," Massie said under her breath.

"I heard that," Layne said.

"Oh, by the way, here's your hat back," Massie said. "Sorry I had it so long."

Chris took the hat and contorted his face. "Smell all that perfume?" he said. "I swear some of the old ladies around here have no idea when to stop."

Alicia, Dylan, and Kristen sauntered into the tent and beelined straight for the band to make a request.

"Are you going to be here for a minute?" Massie asked Chris. "There are a few people I'd like to bring over for you to meet." She turned to walk toward her friends, but Layne stopped her.

"Wait, before you go, there's someone I'd like you to meet." Layne looked past Massie and fixed her gaze on a perfect-looking blonde dressed in head to toe Calvin. She was standing just outside their circle, talking to a group of high school girls. The glowing paper lanterns that hung down from the inside of the tent cast a warm glow on her perfect Clean and Clear commercial skin.

"Fawn," Layne said. "I'd like to introduce you to Massie Block."

The girl turned her head like she was in slow motion, and it seemed like someone had suddenly hit the mute button on the conversations and laughter that had been building around her.

Fawn extended her deeply tanned arm so she could shake Massie's hand.

"You have an amazing house," Fawn said as they shook.

"Thanks," Massie said.

"Fawn is Chris's girlfriend," Layne announced

Massie heard Claire giggle.

"They've been dating since the seventh grade," Layne added.

"Massie's going to teach you how to ride next." Chris gave Fawn a squeeze around her tiny waist when he said it. "Maybe we can all go tomorrow?"

"Maybe," Massie said. She checked her shoe to make sure it wasn't stuck in the grass so she could make a quick getaway. "Let's talk in the morning. I may have plans in the city, but I'll let you know."

Massie gently put Bean on the grass and tiptoed away as quickly as she could.

"Oh, it was nice meeting you, Dawn," she called back over her shoulder.

Massie had ten steps left to figure out what she would

tell her friends when they asked her to introduce them to Chris Abeley—who, by the way, would be known as Chris because he was no longer worthy of firsty-lasty status. Massie *hated* to lose. Losing made her *sick,* but even she knew it could have been worse. If she had to lose to someone, Massie was glad it was Fawn and not, say, Claire.

"I saw you talking to Chris Abeley back there," Alicia teased. "He is *such* a babe."

"Correction—Chris *was* such a babe," Massie said. "He's done."

"Why?" Dylan squealed.

Massie leaned in and the rest of the girls followed.

"I was telling him about that crazy waiter we always get at Panache and he started laughing so hard a booger flew out of his nose and landed on his sleeve," Massie said.

"EEEEEwwwwwww," they yelled.

"Shhhhh," Massie snapped. "I don't want him to know I'm telling you."

"What did you do?" Kristen asked.

"I didn't want to embarrass the poor guy, so I pretended I didn't notice, but I was totally grossed."

"Anyway, it looks like that blonde girl is trying to come on to him," Dylan said.

"Good, she can have him," Massie said. "I've missed out on a lot of shopping trips because of him."

"Yeah, you have a lot of catching up to do," Dylan said.

"In more ways than one." Alicia was looking at the group of four Briarwood boys that was headed their way. She slowly hooked her hair behind one ear and tilted her head so she could keep tabs on the boys without looking like she was.

"Incoming," Dylan said. "I call the one in the yellow tie."

"Wait, I know him," Kristen said. "Isn't that Ben?"

"Ben who?" Dylan asked. There was a trace of jealousy in her voice.

"Ben Zoyl Peroxide," Kristen said.

The girls burst out laughing.

"Gross! His face looks like it's covered in stucco," Alicia said.

"Ewww, it does." Dylan said. "I'm so breaking up with him."

"Now's your chance," Alicia said. "He's heading straight for us."

"So are his ah-dorable friends," Massie said.

She turned her back toward them and swiped some gloss across her lips.

When she turned around again, she spoke with renewed self-confidence, almost like her battery had been recharged.

"We have to look like we're having fun," she said. "So when I count to three, everyone start laughing. Ready? One . . . two . . . three."

Thank God I wore cowboy boots, Claire thought as she watched Massie stumble across the grass and almost bump into a small hors d'oeuvres table. Layne was telling her about the time she walked in on Fawn and Chris making out, but Claire was more interested in Massie and what she was telling her friends, who were huddled close together near the dance floor.

A group of boys cautiously inched their way across the tent toward the girls. They saw the boys coming but pretended they were laughing too hard to care.

Claire was happy she and Layne were friends again, but she couldn't help feeling that she was missing out on something bigger. She shook the thought from her head and tried to tune back into Layne.

"Were the lights off or on?" Claire asked.

"Off, but the TV was on, so I could see everything," Layne said.

The band busted into a rendition of "We Are Family," by Sister Sledge, and Claire watched as the boys got up the nerve to ask Massie and her friends to dance. Claire couldn't tell if the girls were happy to be asked or embarrassed, because they whispered to each other the whole time.

"Why doesn't anyone ask *us* to dance?" Claire asked Layne.

Layne turned to face Claire and bowed deeply. "Claire, would you like to dance?"

"That's not exactly what I had in mind. But okay," Claire said.

They exploded onto the floor and incorporated every move they had ever seen into their routines. Pirouettes, leaps, kick-ball changes, and popping were all represented. A crowd of onlookers gathered around them, laughing at their moves in a good way. Claire and Layne were the center of attention and they couldn't get enough. They ratcheted up their routines by adding dips, spins, and cartwheels so they could keep their viewers interested until the end of the song.

Claire stole a peek at Massie, who was dancing with one of the boys. She looked good when she danced, casual and on beat. During the chorus of the song she bent her elbows and raised her arms above her shoulders. It seemed like she wanted to snap her fingers, but she never did. She never smiled or looked at the boy she was dancing with. She would just look above him or at the ground.

Claire hoped the people watching thought she was more fun than Massie. Maybe one of them would secretly wonder what it would be like to hang out with Claire Lyons.

When the song ended, Claire and Layne curtsied for their audience. The roaring applause made them anxious for the next song to start so they could give the people more of what they wanted. But the band walked off the stage.

"It is better to have danced and lost than never to have

danced at all," Layne said with her hand on her heart. She was out of breath.

"Too true." Claire sighed. "Too true."

Kendra Block climbed the steps to the stage, looking stiffer than the Tin Man from the *Wizard of Oz*. Her silver Chanel heels were so high, she had to walk carefully to avoid a fatal run-in with a pebble or a random twig.

"Ladies and gentlemen, friends of OCD, on behalf of my family I would like to welcome you to the fifth annual benefit auction." She paused for applause. "As always we will be raising money for the OCD scholarship fund" (unexpected applause) "and when you see all of the great stuff we have up for bid, you'll be whipping out your wallets faster than I can say 'sample sale'!" Applause. "I'm going to pass the microphone over to Kevin Ambrose so we can get this party started! Woo-hooo!" Kendra shot her fist in the air and tilted her head down rock-star style.

"Oh my God, if I was Massie, I'd be so mortified right now," Claire said.

"Look." Layne pointed toward Massie. Her head was buried in Alicia's collarbone; she was probably praying for the moment to pass. "Even the cool girls have embarrassing parents."

"All righty, folks, the first item up for grabs is this five-speed electronic back massager," Kevin said. "I'm going to start the bidding at ten dollars."

"This is going to be a long night." Layne sighed. "What do you want to do?"

"We can go hang out in my room. I just want to wait and see what my stuff goes for," Claire said.

Layne sighed and took a long sip of her virgin cosmopolitan.

After twenty-five minutes of household appliances, CDs, and computer software Kevin moved on to the clothes.

Claire's sweatshirts sold for fifty cents apiece to Rose Goldberg, who said they'd be great for polishing silver.

"There, can we go now?" Layne asked.

"My fancy stuff is next, hold on," Claire said to Layne without looking at her. All she could focus on was her DKNY dress, her beaded bag, and her Marc Jacobs heels that Kevin hung over the front of his podium.

"Those are *yours?*" Layne widened her eyes.

Claire scratched her arm. "Alicia bought them for me that one day we were friends."

"I can't believe you're getting rid of them!"

"The dress was so tight it gave me gas and the shoes gave me blisters."

"*So?*" Layne shook her head, confused.

"Plus I get to see *that.*" Claire pointed to Alicia.

Her arms were tightly folded across her chest and her bottom teeth were covering her top teeth, which made her look like a bulldog.

"Look how mad she is," Layne said. "What are you going to do?"

"It depends," Claire said.

"On what?" Layne asked.

"What she does."

Alicia stormed across the dance floor and marched over to Claire. Dylan was beside her.

"You have no right to auction that outfit," Alicia fumed. "It's mine and I want it back."

"Then you better start bidding," Claire said.

Layne would have jumped in to defend her friend, but she had lost her ability to speak. Claire knew Layne was surprised by her defiance and liked being thought of as tough and fiery.

"Two hundred dollars," a voice called out from the crowd.

"Three-fifty," another said.

Claire was proud of herself for choosing an outfit that was in such high demand.

"Four twenty-five."

"Do I hear five hundred?" Kevin asked.

"Six hundred dollars," Claire shouted.

"Do I hear six-fifty?" Kevin said.

It was silent.

"Six hundred going once, going twice, *sold* to the lady in the cowboy boots," Kevin said as he slammed his gavel on the podium.

The only sound Claire could hear was her heart beating and her favorite cowboy boots stepping on the grass below her feet while she walked to pick up her dress.

She handed Kevin a manila envelope stuffed with twenty-dollar bills and grabbed her outfit and her I SUPPORT OCD pin.

Claire winked at her parents. They'd been really upset

when they first found out she'd let Alicia buy her the outfit. Her mother had insisted she pay Alicia back with the money in her savings account. But after a long discussion Claire had gotten her parents to agree to *this* plan instead. This way Alicia got the outfit back and the money went to charity. And all was well.

"Here's your precious outfit back." Claire tossed the clothes at Alicia as she walked by. She wished she had paused to see her reaction, but she couldn't stop. The adrenaline wouldn't let her.

Claire finally stopped moving when she got to the back of the tent and realized she had nowhere left to go. She leaned against the thick canvas walls, hoping Layne would rescue her so they could leave. There was no way she was going to stick around the party after she'd one-upped Alicia in public. That would be social suicide.

Layne was talking to a cute busboy and Claire did her best to send telepathic cries for help.

Come on, Layne. Let's go, Layne. LAYNE! But nothing worked.

The sound of microphone feedback pierced the air and everyone looked over at the stage as if they had just been woken up from a deep sleep.

"Sorry 'bout that, folks," William Block snickered. He was swaying back and forth so much, Claire knew he had to be drunk. She snuck a peek at Chris Abeley just to see if he had noticed it. He had. His hand was over his face and his head was shaking back and forth. Claire could tell he was thinking, *Here we go again,* and she was anxious to find out what William would do next.

"I'd like to call an old buddy of mine onstage so he can help me out with the next item up for b-hiccup-id," he said.

"Jay Lyons, everyone." Claire's eyes widened and her face shot forward as if someone had surprised her with a slap on the back. She didn't dare look at Chris this time.

"Hello, everyone," he said. Claire didn't think he seemed any more sober than William.

"Now, here's what we're gonna do." He placed his arm around Jay so slowly it looked like they were moving underwater.

"All we need is one thousand dollars more and OCD will have a new scholarship. Sooo, Jay and I are going to sing 'Ninety-nine Bottles of Beer on the Wall'—"

"Is that how much you drank tonight?" someone shouted. Everyone laughed.

William ignored the heckler and continued explaining his plan.

"And we're not going to stop singing until we get the money," he said.

Hands started clapping in anticipation of a beat. The crowd was anxious to see these two grown men make fools of themselves, like bloodthirsty spectators at a boxing match.

"I want my family up here," Jay said.

To everyone's delight, Todd ran up onstage and started dancing around like a maniac.

"Where's my daughter? Claire? Claire? Come on up here!"

Claire's mouth tasted like pennies again, which was a sign that puke was right around the corner. She could not believe her father was doing this, not only to himself but to her! Didn't he understand that she had enough problems?

When she heard her name a third time, she ran outside the tent and took cover in a patch of azaleas.

It wasn't until they got to ninety-one bottles that Mr. Block started calling for Massie. Once he started, he couldn't stop. "Where's my angel?" he called into the microphone. "Massie, come up here and help us out. It's your school, honey. It's all for you!"

Claire glanced over at Massie who was standing alone by the stage, looking uncomfortable. In that single moment Claire saw something in Massie that both amazed and confused her. Massie looked embarrassed, desperate, and scared. Massie looked human.

Claire reached into her pocket and pulled out Mr. Rivera's cell phone. She'd fully intended to give it back to Alicia with the dress, but in the heat of the moment she forgot.

CLAIRE: TAKE COVER. GO 2 THE AZAYLAYAAAAZ

"Where's my little baby?" Mr. Block said again into the microphone.

Claire was wondering the same thing. She tried to peek through the bushes to find Massie, but all she could see was the back of the bartender standing next to crates of dirty glasses and empty bottles. She checked her screen, but Massie never responded. She was mad at herself for expecting otherwise.

CLAIRE: HURRY!

The dads were down to eighty-nine and showed no signs of tiring out anytime soon. She would gladly have given them the money they needed if she hadn't just blown it on an outfit she couldn't keep.

MASSIE: TAKE CARE OF BEAN IF I DON'T MAKE IT
CLAIRE: LOL

"Move over," Massie whispered from somewhere in the darkness. "Oh my God, this is brutal." She was out of breath when she plopped herself down in the dirt beside Claire.

"I know. Parents shouldn't be allowed near alcohol." Claire rolled her eyes.

"Or microphones." Massie smirked.

Both girls laughed awkwardly and spent the next few seconds drowning in unbearable silence.

"What would you rather," Claire finally said. "Go up onstage and sing 'Ninety-nine Bottles' with our dads or hide in the bushes all night and get attacked by ants?"

"I think we both know the answer to that one," Massie said. "And hey, there's always oatmeal if our bites get really severe."

"Wait. Really? That was you?" Claire said. "Thanks."

She pulled a Ziploc bag filled with gummies out of her side pocket and held it open for Massie.

"You want?" Claire offered.

"Yeah, totally," Massie said. She took the piece of pink gum out of her mouth and wrapped it up in a leaf and buried it in the dirt. Claire watched her navigate around the inside of the bag, trying to avoid contact with the green ones.

"I thought you hated gummies," Claire said. She wasn't trying to start a fight. She was genuinely curious about Massie's change of heart. "Did you skip dinner or something?"

"No, I love gummies," Massie admitted. "I just hate what they do to my thighs. See, you're lucky you don't have that problem. You're a twig."

Claire looked at Massie's charm bracelet as it batted around the inside of the bag.

"I can't believe you're actually wearing the charm my parents bought you." Claire shook her head.

"Oh yeah. Well, it's cute," Massie offered.

"Really? I thought you'd hate it," Claire said. "I told my parents to go with the gold crown or the letter *M* but they insisted on the microphone because they said you used to like singing."

"The truth is, I kind of did." Massie gave Claire a tiny, genuine smile. "I actually went through a phase where I really liked musicals. I'd lock myself in the sauna room and sing songs from *Annie* and *Pippin*."

"Are you *serious?*"

"If you tell anyone, I'll make your life miserable," Massie said, but she was kidding. Sort of. The two girls spent the next two hours hiding in the azaleas talking about TV shows, celebrity crushes, favorite Web sites, and disgusting smells.

They didn't even hear their fathers cheering because they got all the money by the time they hit sixty-eight. They finally tuned in to the party once it was all over and the band was saying good night.

"Well, I guess it's safe to come out of hiding now," Claire said. She didn't realize how chilly she was until she stood up.

Massie and Claire faced each other. Even though they had just talked for hours, they were both speechless. Claire wondered if this was what the awkward is-he-going-to-kiss-me-good-night moment at the end of a date was like. If it was, she hoped she'd never be in a position to find out.

"Well," Massie said. She slid her charm bracelet up and down her arm. "Thanks for saving me tonight." She dropped her gaze toward her pointy shoes and massaged her temples with one hand. Her troubled expression reminded Claire of an actress, desperately searching her memory for a forgotten line. "I had fun."

I had fun.

I had fun.

I had fun.

Those words played over and over again in Claire's mind while she got ready for bed. When she was finally under the warm covers, she reached for her Elph and scrolled through her pictures. She raced past the shots of OCD, Layne, expensive price tags, and celebrity-size mansions until she found the shot she was looking for. The one she'd taken of herself the night of the sleepover at Massie's, the one she'd decided to call "Rock Bottom."

The night she'd taken it, she made a promise to herself. And by looking at the image of her sad eyes, she was keeping it. It was supposed to remind her not to ever, under any circumstances, believe that she and Massie could be real friends.

Only this time she had a feeling things were different.

Of course Claire wouldn't know for sure until Monday.

Massie dried off after her twenty-five-minute steaming hot shower and slipped into her purple silk pajamas. Her body ached from sitting cross-legged for three hours and her insides were still chilled, even though her skin was red from the scalding water. She sat down on her bed and scratched Bean behind the ears.

"Well, Bean," she said. "Only one thing left to do."

CURRENT STATE OF THE UNION	
IN	**OUT**
MOTHERS	FATHERS
CUTE BOY ON DANCE FLOOR	CHRIS ABELEY
WITH DORKY LOAFERS	
CLAIRE	CLAIRE

Massie spent twenty minutes longer than she wanted on her State of the Union because she didn't know where to put Claire. She wasn't exactly "out" anymore, but she certainly wasn't "in." When Massie thought about how hard they'd laughed in the bushes, she moved Claire to the "in" column. But when she remembered how annoying it was to have a tagalong, she put her in the "out" column. Finally, when she couldn't stay awake any longer, she came up with a suitable plan. She would start a W.A.S. column for times like these when she would simply have to *wait and see*. That way she could take her time and decide next week.